D0502031

THE BOBBSEY TWINS AND THE FOUR-LEAF CLOVER MYSTERY

"Purple footprints!" exclaimed Freddie Bobbsey. Do they belong to the vanishing prowler? How could the soldier disappear from a locked room? Who stole the hex signs and caused the twins' canoe accident?

Puzzling questions like these and exciting adventures send the four Bobbsey Twins on a search for a golden birthday present.

Readers, see if you can solve the hundred-year-old mystery of Cloverbank Farm along with Nan, Bert, Freddie, and Flossie. You'll have "wonderful good" fun!

THE BOBBSEY TWINS

By Laura Lee Hope

The Bobbsey Twins of Lakeport
- Adventure in the Country
- The Secret at the Seashore
- Mystery at School
- And the Mystery at Snow Lodge
- On a Houseboat
- Mystery at Meadowbrook
- Big Adventure at Home
- Search in the Great City
- On Blueberry Island
- Mystery on the Deep Blue Sea
- Adventure in Washington
- Visit to the Great West
- And the Cedar Camp Mystery
- And the County Fair Mystery
- Camping Out
- Adventures with Baby May
- And the Play House Secret
- And the Four-Leaf Clover Mystery
- Wonderful Winter Secret
- And the Circus Surprise
- Solve a Mystery
- In the Land of Cotton
- At Mystery Mansion
- In Tulip Land
- In Rainbow Valley
- Own Little Railroad
- At Whitesail Harbor
- And the Horseshoe Riddle
- At Big Bear Pond
- On a Bicycle Trip
- Own Little Ferryboat
- At Pilgrim Rock
- Forest Adventure
- At London Tower
- In the Mystery Cave
- In Volcano Land
- The Goldfish Mystery
- And the Big River Mystery
- And the Greek Hat Mystery
- Search for the Green Rooster
- And Their Camel Adventure
- Mystery of the King's Puppet
- And the Secret of Candy Castle
- And the Doodlebug Mystery

"These are the young detectives who solved the mystery."

The Bobbsey Twins and the Four-Leaf Clover Mystery

By

LAURA LEE HOPE

GROSSET & DUNLAP

Publishers *New York*

PRINTED IN THE UNITED STATES OF AMERICA
LIBRARY OF CONGRESS CATALOG CARD NO. 68-29948
The Bobbsey Twins and the Four-Leaf Clover Mystery

CONTENTS

THE BOBBSEY TWINS AND THE FOUR-LEAF CLOVER MYSTERY

CHAPTER I

THE MYSTERY ROOM

"WATCH OUT, Henry! You're getting us all wet!" cried Bert Bobbsey.

"Aim the hose the other way!" called his dark-haired twin Nan. They were twelve.

The boy in the yard grinned and threw another shower of spray over the five children on the front porch of Cloverbank farmhouse. Freddie and Flossie Bobbsey, the six-year-old blond twins, squealed and jumped out of the way.

"You stop that, Henry Zoop!" cried Nellie Parks, his cousin, who was Nan's best friend. "Aunt Doris only told you to show us around!"

"You can go on home for all I care," said ten-year-old Henry. "We don't need any more detectives here. I'll solve the mysteries myself."

The Bobbseys' eyes lighted up. They loved mysteries!

"How did you know we were detectives?" Freddie asked.

"Nellie wrote me all about you," Henry replied.

"What are your mysteries?" Flossie spoke up.

"I'm not telling," said Henry, hitching up his shorts. He was a thin boy with knobby knees and straight hair. "Just remember *I'm* the detective around here, and I don't want anybody butting in on my cases."

"That's a terrible way to talk to your guests, Henry," said Nellie sternly.

"I don't care," her cousin replied.

Henry's parents had invited Nellie and the Bobbseys to visit the Zoops' big farm in Pennsylvania Dutch country for their spring vacation. That afternoon the five children had flown from their hometown of Lakeport to Lancaster, where Henry's father had picked them up in his station wagon.

"Supper will be ready soon," said a cheerful voice. The children turned to see Nellie's Aunt Doris at the screen door. She was a tall woman, blond and pretty, wearing a flowered apron.

"Henry, show our guests their rooms." She turned to the visitors. "Uncle Walter took your bags up the back way." She hurried off.

After putting the hose away, Henry led the children into the gray stone farmhouse and up a red-carpeted stairway to a long hall. There were four rooms on each side. He opened the second door to the right.

"You girls will be in here," he said.

"Oh, it's bee-yoo-ti-ful!" exclaimed Flossie as they stepped into a big room with pink flowered wallpaper. On one side were three shiny brass beds with gay quilts on them.

"We're at the end of the hall," Henry said to the boys. "Come on."

Taking a guess, Freddie skipped to the last door on the left side.

"Stop!" said Henry quickly. "Don't go in there!"

"Why?" asked Freddie.

"Because that's the mystery room."

"What do you mean?" Bert asked.

"If you go in, you might disappear. And you wouldn't be the first person it happened to."

Freddie's eyes grew big as saucers. "Disappear? You mean like magic?"

"Sure. You could vanish right into thin air," said Henry with a grin.

The girls heard him and came to their door to listen.

"We don't believe in magic," said Bert, smiling, "and I'll bet you don't either. Is this one of your mysteries?"

"It's my number-two mystery," said Henry.

"What's number one?" Nan asked.

Henry bit his lip and shook his head hard.

"I think you're mean," said Nellie.

Her cousin blushed. "No, I'm not!" he replied quickly. "I'm glad you're here. I just don't want you to work on my mysteries."

As he opened the end door on the right, the hinges squeaked. The boys stepped into a big, airy room with colorful maps on the walls.

"I'll take the cot," said Henry. "You can have the bunk beds."

A short time later he led the visitors down to the dining room. They took seats at a large round table set with a white cloth and blue dishes. Mr. Zoop, a friendly, broad-shouldered man with brown hair, said grace.

Then his wife smiled at the twins. "We want you to feel at home," she said, "so you call us Aunt Doris and Uncle Walter, the same as Nellie does."

As they ate a hearty meal, Henry told the other children that he had a pet sheep named Sheela. "And I have something else," he added mysteriously.

"An elephant?" asked Freddie jokingly.

Henry laughed. "Smaller."

"A tame flea," said Bert with a grin.

"I'll give you a hint," said Henry. "A-B-C-letter ten in a tree."

The visitors puzzled for a few moments, then Nan smiled and said, "I know."

Bert laughed and nodded.

Quickly Flossie counted on her fingers. "The tenth letter of the alphabet is J."

"That's the mystery room," said Henry

"J in a tree!" Freddie burst out. "It's a bird! A blue jay!"

When supper was over, Henry took them through the cheerful kitchen and out onto the long back porch. A large oak grew nearby. On a low limb sat a blue jay. Henry gave a short whistle and the bird flew onto his head.

"Oh, how cute!" exclaimed Nellie, clapping her hands.

"Hello there, Jiffy," said Henry and gave the jay a bit of bread.

"How long have you had him?" Nan asked.

"Since we moved here last winter. I found him with a broken leg. Daddy helped me fix it." The bird cocked a bright black eye at the children.

"I have a pony, too," Henry added, "Come on, I'll show you." As he walked off the porch, the jay flew back to the tree.

Henry headed across the big backyard to a wide green hillside where dozens of sheep were grazing. He leaned over the white picket fence and whistled. A shiny brown pony came trotting over.

"Her name's Daisy," said Henry as the visitors petted the animal. "She pulls a cart."

"Let's give her some grass," said Flossie, reaching through the fence to pull a handful.

"It's clover," said Henry. "This whole bank is

full of it. That's how the farm got the name, Cloverbank."

"Oh, maybe we can find a four-leaf clover for luck," said Flossie and began to look through the green leaves in her hand. "Here's one!" She gasped. "And another one!" Her eyes grew round with surprise. "These are all four-leaf clovers!" Amazed, the other children crowded around to look.

"That's funny," said Bert. "They're usually hard to find." He crouched down and looked through the fence. "There's a big patch of them here!"

As Flossie fed her handful to Daisy, Nan grinned. "You're going to have a very lucky pony, Henry."

While the others played with the animal Freddie wandered off toward the big red barn He noticed a round sign on the wall with a blue-and-yellow-and-orange star on it. "That's pretty," he thought, as he opened the barn door and stepped inside.

It was gloomy and smelled of hay. Freddie heard a noise and glanced over at a big barrel. The next moment a man's head popped up out of it. Freddie gasped. The man, who was blond and wore horn-rimmed glasses, ducked down again.

Freddie, frightened, ran back and told the others.

"The prowler again!" exclaimed Henry. "Let's get him!"

The six children dashed to the barn and searched cautiously. It was empty.

"The fellow's slippery," said Henry and explained that he had glimpsed the intruder several times in the last week. "He's a big, tall fellow. Last night I watched from my window and saw him sneaking around here. He's my number-one mystery," he admitted as they left the barn.

Just then Henry's parents came out to the back porch. The children ran over and told about the prowler.

"I wonder who he is and what he wants," said Uncle Walter.

"Have you had anything stolen?" Nan asked.

"No," said Aunt Doris. "But a store in Lebanon was robbed a couple of weeks ago."

"The two men who took the shop's money must be hundreds of miles from here by now," said Uncle Walter. "It's not likely our prowler is one of them."

Henry sighed. "I'd like to catch him. But he always vanishes. Just like people do in the mystery room."

"Now Henry, as far as we know, only one person ever disappeared from there," said Uncle Walter.

"Please tell us about it," Nan said.

Aunt Doris replied, "It was a very long time ago, during the American Revolution."

"That was when George Washington and the Colonists fought the British for our independence," Henry explained to the young twins.

"When the United States was born," Bert added.

"That's right," Henry went on. "And did you know that the British hired some German soldiers to fight us? They were called Hessians." He grinned. "But a number of them ran away from the British Redcoats and joined the Americans."

"This story is about a Hessian," said Aunt Doris.

She went on to tell that the Cloverbank house had been built nearly two hundred years before by a farmer named Scott. One rainy night, he and his wife had gone to help a sick neighbor. Their two children, Betsy, who was twelve, and ten-year-old Ben, were home alone.

"Suddenly they heard pounding on the door. When the children opened it, a Hessian soldier burst in and begged them to hide him from the Redcoats."

"The Scotts were loyal Americans, of course," put in Uncle Walter.

"Betsy and Ben put the Hessian in the mystery room," said Henry. "A few minutes later the

Redcoats arrived. They saw the soldier's muddy footprints on the stairs and followed them to the room. The door was bolted on the inside, so the British broke it open. No one was in there!"

"Besides," said Aunt Doris, "the only window was locked, and there was a big fire in the fireplace, so he didn't go up the chimney."

"Where did the Hessian go?" Flossie asked.

Henry laughed. "That's what the Redcoats wanted to know. They searched the house, but they didn't find him."

"There must be a secret exit in that room," said Nellie.

"Course there is," Henry agreed. "Everybody knows that, but nobody's been able to find it."

Nan's eyes sparkled. "Maybe your two mysteries are connected, Henry. That prowler might be looking for an outside opening to the passage."

"I'd like to know why," said Bert. "Come on, Henry, let us help you solve this case."

The younger boy stuck out his jaw and thrust his hands into his pockets. "I don't want any help."

"Now Henry," his mother said, "you must let your guests have some fun too."

Uncle Walter agreed, then added, "I'll telephone the police and report the prowler now."

After Henry's parents had gone into the

house, he sat sulking on the swing. Then he walked off by himself into the barn.

The Bobbseys and Nellie played tag until dark. Henry came in later, but would not say what he had been doing.

That night Bert was awakened by the squeaking of the bedroom door. He saw Henry slip out with a flashlight. Minutes went by. On a hunch Bert got up and looked out the window. In the moonlight he saw the boy heading toward the barn.

"I wonder what he's up to," Bert thought.

Just then Freddie awakened. "What's the matter?" he asked sleepily.

Bert told him. "Let's follow Henry."

The brothers put on slippers and robes. Taking their own flashlights, they hurried downstairs and out the back way to the barn.

Cautiously Bert opened the big door and stepped inside. The next moment something caught him by the ankle and jerked him off his feet!

CHAPTER II

A GOLDEN GIFT

WITH a yell Bert sat down hard on the ground. But his one foot was held up in the air!

"Bert! What happened?" Freddie cried, rushing into the barn. His flashlight showed a rope around Bert's ankle.

A moment later another flashlight was turned on. "You spoiled it all!" exclaimed Henry's voice.

"You mean you set this trap?" asked Bert angrily.

"Course! But not for you. For the prowler."

Henry took the noose off Bert's ankle. Then he showed the boys how he had laid it on the floor by the door and looped the other end of the rope over the front of an empty stall. "I hid inside it. As soon as I heard somebody come in, I pulled the rope."

Bert grunted as he got to his feet. "Too bad you didn't wait to see who it was."

"You made so much noise, it probably scared the prowler off," Henry grumbled. The Bobbseys agreed, and the three went back to bed.

The next morning the children had breakfast together at the big table in the kitchen. As they were finishing, there was a noise on the porch and a low "Baa." A large white sheep stood outside the screen door.

"Hi, Sheela girl!" exclaimed Henry as he jumped up. He opened the door and the animal walked into the kitchen. She stopped at the table and looked expectantly at Nan, who was putting jam on toast.

"Oh, she's darling!" Flossie cried. The little girl wriggled off the chair and threw her arms around the woolly sheep.

"She's so tame!" exclaimed Nellie.

"And very spoiled!" added Aunt Doris. She clapped her hands at the pet. "Come on, Sheela, outside now!"

But the sheep's long lip had closed over the piece of jam toast which Nan had fed her and she was munching contentedly.

"Let's go, Sheela," said Henry. He grasped the sheep's red collar and led her outside into a wire pen under the big oak. The other children followed and watched as the sheep went into a shelter at the back and began to eat from a bin.

"The wire is loose and she keeps getting out," said Henry, as he closed the gate. "She loves to come in the house—especially during storms, 'cause she's scared of thunder. We have cows, too," he went on. "They're in our low meadow." He pointed toward the side of the yard away from the barn. "You can't see it from here. It's out past those two small stone houses."

"What's in those?" Nellie asked.

"Nothing now," Henry replied. "One's the old spring house. Years ago, people stored milk there to keep it cool. The other is where all the baking was done. It's ruined," he added, "but Daddy's going to fix it up. Same as the smokehouse." He nodded toward a small building beside the barn. "Come on, I'll show you the cows."

"Later, Henry," said Nan quickly. "Right now we'd better get started with our detective work."

Henry looked sulky, but he followed the visitors to the mystery room. It was large, with whitewashed walls. Blue curtains in the window matched the coverlet on the big wooden bed. On the inside wall was a fireplace made of huge stones.

The twins and Nellie searched but found no hidden exit in the walls, floor, or ceiling.

"Let's examine the fireplace too," Nan said.

"What's the use?" Nellie objected. "After all, there was a fire in it when the soldier disappeared. He couldn't have crawled through the flames."

"It won't hurt to check anyway," said Bert.

The children tested each stone, inside and out. Not one was loose.

"Who owned this house before you did?" Nan asked Henry.

"Otto Hummel. He lives about a mile from here in a big barn. He paints hex signs for people to nail to their barns." The boy added that these were round, colorful decorations like the one painted on the Zoops' barn.

"I think we ought to go see Mr. Hummel," said Nan. "Maybe he can help us."

Henry trailed along as the detectives went downstairs and told Aunt Doris. She said, "Walk straight along the highway. You can't miss the place."

Henry did not want to go, but as Nellie and the Bobbseys went down the drive, they saw him watching from the front porch.

"I wish Henry didn't feel bad because we're helping with the mysteries," Nan remarked. "If we worked together, everybody could have fun."

After a while Flossie called out, "There it is!" and pointed to a large yellow barn on top of a hill. All over the sides were colorful hex signs showing flowers, stars, and birds.

The children hurried up the winding drive to

the open door. Outside was a table with large wooden hex signs stacked on it.

"They're bee-yoo-ti-ful!" exclaimed Flossie as her twin picked one up.

"No, Freddie!" said Nan quickly. Startled, the boy dropped the round sign and it went rolling down the drive.

"Catch it!" Nan cried as her brothers plunged for the disc. Bert grabbed it and returned the sign to the table.

"Don't touch anything more," said Nan sternly to her little brother.

The visitors stepped to the open barn door. Inside was a big white-haired man seated at a long worktable. He looked up from the sign he was painting.

"What I can do for you?" he asked with a smile.

Nan introduced herself and the others. "Are you Mr. Hummel?"

"*Ja,* but everybody calls me Otto, so you do that, too."

"These are cool signs," said Freddie, glancing at the hundreds stacked around the barn.

Bert added, "I read once that some of the Pennsylvania Dutch farmers are superstitious and use them to scare witches away from their barns."

Otto shook his head so hard, his short curls

"Catch it!" Nan cried

jiggled. "No, no, no! Hex signs are not for that! They're chust for pretty."

As the children smiled, Otto's blue eyes danced. *"Ja.* I talk funny—with a German accent. You see, we are not really Dutch. Our ancestors came from Germany over."

Flossie beamed. "It's fun to hear you talk."

"What that?" Freddie asked, looking at the funny yellow bird the man was painting.

"A *distelfink,"* he said.

The children laughed.

"A what kind of fink?" Bert asked.

Otto grinned. *"Distelfink.* That's Pennsylvania Dutch for Thistle Finch. These birds use thistledown to make their nests. Another name is goldfinch. They're supposed to bring good luck. Did you come to buy a sign?"

"No, we're detectives," said Freddie, and Nan asked if he knew where the secret passage was at Cloverbank.

"Ach no! Everybody in my family tried to find it. Nobody did." He went on to explain that he was a bachelor and the last of the Hummels. "My great-grandfather, John Hummel, bought Cloverbank from the Scott family—the first owners."

The children now told him about the prowler they had seen.

Otto's bushy brows shot up. "That sounds like Dr. Fox."

"Who's he?" asked Freddie.

"A professor from a big university—or that's what he said. He came to my shop last week and told me he was writing a book on old houses with secret passageways. He wanted to know about Cloverbank. So I told him the story of the golden birthday present."

Otto put down his brush. "Now I'll tell you. Have a *sitz,"* he added, pointing to the bench on the other side of the table. Smiling, the children guessed what he meant and sat down.

Otto said that two days after his great-grandfather had bought Cloverbank, the Civil War had broken out. "That's when the North and South fought each other," he explained to Freddie and Flossie, "and Abraham Lincoln was the President."

The children nodded. "Did your great-grandfather fight in the war?" Bert asked.

"Ja. Right away he went in the Union Army. Well, he was afraid the fighting might come to Pennsylvania, so he sent his wife and ten children to stay with relatives in Canada.

"The day after his family left, a present arrived for the children from their Uncle Fritz, who was a goldsmith in Germany. He could never keep the ten birthdays straight, so each year he sent one gift for all of them."

"What was it?" Freddie asked eagerly.

Otto shrugged. "Nobody knows exactly.

Great-grandfather wrote to his family to say that he was keeping the gift as a surprise for them. He had found a very special hiding place for it. He gave them one hint, though. He said Uncle Fritz had written a letter saying that he had made the golden toy himself and it would be fun for Pennsylvania children."

"You mean no one has ever seen it?" Nellie asked.

"No. Great-grandfather died in the war and soon afterward Uncle Fritz died in Germany. When Great-grandmother and the children returned they could not find the present anywhere. It hasn't been found to this day."

Bert's eyes were full of excitement. "I'll bet the prowler was looking for that birthday present!"

"Maybe John Hummel hid it in the secret passage," said Nan.

"Could be," said the hex artist, "but if Great-grandfather knew about a way out of that room, he never informed his family. They didn't hear about the passage until long after they had come from Canada back. Then an old neighbor told them the story of the Hessian."

The children said the Zoops had told them about the soldier. They thanked Otto and hurried back to Cloverbank. The kitchen was empty, but they could smell something baking.

"We'd better get ready for lunch," said Nan.

The girls went upstairs but soon returned to the kitchen. It was still empty.

"Maybe Aunt Doris is outside," said Flossie. "I'll look."

She skipped outside and around to the front of the house. No one was in sight. As she paused by the steps, she heard a loud *achoo!*

"That sounded as if it came from under the porch," Flossie thought.

She stooped down and peered through the wooden lattice into the dark space underneath. At first she could see nothing, then she noticed a big black shape crouched on the ground. With a terrible growl, it moved toward her.

CHAPTER III

PURPLE PRINTS

FLOSSIE screamed and ran around the side of the house.

Nan and Nellie heard her and dashed outdoors to see what the trouble was.

"There's a big black thing under the porch!" cried Flossie.

Nan put an arm around the frightened child. "Are you sure you didn't imagine it?" she asked kindly.

The little girl shook her head hard. "I'm positive!"

"Maybe it was Henry," said Nellie. "He'd think it was funny to scare us."

"You probably saw a dog," Nan said.

"No. It was real big," Flossie quavered.

"Well, let's go see," said Nan.

She took Flossie's hand and led the way to the front of the house.

"Look!" exclaimed Nan, pointing to a section

of the lattice which was lying flat on the ground. "That's how the creature got in and out."

"Maybe it's still under there," whispered Flossie.

The girls stooped in front of the opening and peered into the gloom. They could see nothing.

"Come on!" said Nan. She crawled inside and the others followed. The ground was damp and soft. "Look!" Nan said softly. "Here's a hand print!"

"Somebody was crawling around in here, all right," said Nellie. "See the marks on the ground."

"Whoever it was probably sneaked out while Flossie was telling us about him," said Nan.

"I'll bet it was the bad man," said her sister.

"We'd better tell the others," Nellie remarked.

The girls crawled out from under the porch. As they put back the section of lattice, Nan noticed a small piece of paper lying beside the steps. She picked it up. Printed on it in pencil were the words: ALBERT MEYER. CHEESES—LANCASTER MARKET.

"Is that a clue?" Nellie asked eagerly.

"If Dr. Fox dropped it," Nan replied. "Maybe Mr. Meyer can tell us where Dr. Fox is staying. Then we could tell the police."

Excited by their find, the girls hurried to the back yard. They found Uncle Walter and the three boys mending the chicken coop which stood at the far side of the barn.

"Henry, were you under the front porch a little while ago?" Nellie asked her cousin.

"No. Why?"

As the girls told what had happened, Aunt Doris came out of the barn wearing a smock and carrying a paste brush.

"Dr. Fox must have parked his car at the foot of the hill among the trees," Nan finished, "and then sneaked up the drive."

"I'll report this to the police right away," Uncle Walter said and strode off.

"You have a good clue," Aunt Doris remarked. "I'm going to market in Lancaster tomorrow. Would you like to go along and question the cheese man?"

"That would be neat!" exclaimed Bert.

After lunch Henry invited the boys to go fishing. "There's a big creek," he told them, "up in the woods behind the barn."

"Why don't you girls visit the museum down the road?" Aunt Doris suggested. "You'll have fun there. I'd go with you, but I'm restoring some nice old traveling trunks I found out here."

Ten minutes later, the girls walked up onto the porch of a large white frame dwelling. A sign beside the door said: THE OLD-TIME HOUSE.

In front of the sill was a hooked rug with the word *Villkom* on it.

"That must mean Welcome in Pennsylvania Dutch," said Nan.

Nellie rang the bell. A moment later the door was opened by a pretty young woman wearing a Colonial costume. She had curly brown hair which peeked out from beneath her starched white cap. With a little curtsy, she invited them in. "My name is Lulu Bumiller," she added. "Just call me Miss Lulu."

Smiling, the girls stepped into the large front room. In the center was a big wooden table. A bright, round braided rug covered the wide floorboards. At one side was a big brick fireplace with a spinning wheel in front of it.

"Oh it's just like a picture!" Nan exclaimed.

Flossie clapped her hands. "Everything is old-timey." She looked at the girl. "Even you!"

The hostess laughed. "Well I'm not quite as old as the house," she said. "Would you like to look around?"

"We'd love to," said Nellie.

Nan saw a little box beside the door marked *admission* and put in enough money for three. Then Miss Lulu led them upstairs into a bedroom where there was a high four-poster with a canopy. On the bed lay a beautiful quilt made of pieces of red and blue velvet.

"There are pictures of children on it!" exclaimed Flossie as she looked at the coverlet. Girls in sunbonnets and long dresses were embroidered in white silk thread.

"This quilt is very old," Miss Lulu told them. "It belonged to my great-great-grandmother."

"Was this her house?" Nellie asked.

Miss Lulu nodded. "The Bumillers have lived here since the Revolution."

"Then maybe you could help us," said Nan. She explained about the mystery they were working on. "Do you know where the secret passage is at Cloverbank Farm?"

"I'm afraid not," said Miss Lulu. "I'm sure the Scotts built it for escape during Indian attacks. They never would admit there was a tunnel. I guess they thought it safer not to tell about it."

"Are there any of that family left who might know?" Nan asked.

"No," replied Miss Lulu. "They've all been gone a long time."

As the girls thanked her, Flossie noticed a wooden cradle with two tulips painted on it. "How pretty!"

"Yes," said Miss Lulu. "Those flowers are on many pieces of furniture here, because there were always lots of tulips growing around this house." She explained that many Pennsylvania

Dutch families had favorite designs which they used in their homes.

After finishing the upstairs tour, Miss Lulu led the girls down to the big kitchen. She served them each a thick slice of warm homemade bread with butter and preserves.

"I made the butter myself," said Miss Lulu, pointing to a large churn which stood in the corner.

"It's yummy," said Flossie, and the other girls agreed.

Just then the front doorbell rang.

"I'll go," said Flossie and skipped off to open the door.

On the threshold stood a tall, dark-haired man with a black mustache. He stared at Flossie for an instant and then said that he would like to see Miss Bumiller. "My name is Mr. Drucker."

Miss Lulu came up behind Flossie with Nan and Nellie. Drucker explained that he was writing a book on the Pennsylvania Dutch country. "I'd like some information about the Cloverbank house," he added.

As the other girls looked at him sharply, Flossie stared at his trousers. The knees had bits of dark earth on them!

Flossie gasped. "You're the bad man!" she blurted. "We've been looking for you!"

Mr. Drucker turned pale. Without a word, he

hurried down the porch steps. Nan and Nellie ran over in time to see him drive off in a black sedan.

"Do you really think he was the prowler?" asked Miss Lulu.

"Yes, 'cause he had muddy knees from hiding under the porch," said Flossie.

"But he wasn't blond like Dr. Fox," Nellie put in.

Nan looked thoughtful. "This man was big, though, the way Henry said the prowler was. I think he had on a wig and a false mustache."

Miss Lulu nodded. "It is unlikely that two men should be writing books about Cloverbank house."

"He probably got a disguise because Freddie saw him," Nan added.

"Never mind about *that!*" Nellie exclaimed. "He's seen *us* now and knows we're after him."

"Yes, you must be very careful," said Miss Lulu. "He may be dangerous."

The children promised, then hurried back to the farm. The three boys were in the kitchen cleaning fish while Aunt Doris melted the fat in a deep skillet. While it sizzled, the girls told their story.

Bert patted his little sister on the shoulder. "Good work, Floss. I'm glad you noticed those muddy knees."

Flossie beamed proudly.

"You're the bad man!" Flossie blurted

"Aw, that's nothing," said Henry. "You didn't catch the fellow, and that's what I'm going to do!"

"Now, Henry," said Aunt Doris, "don't brag."

"Well, I am," Henry insisted, "and if you don't believe it just come and look at my latest trap."

He led the visitors to the back of the barn. He pointed to several branches lying on the ground.

"That's my Prowler Pit," Henry announced. "If that fellow comes sneaking around here and steps on those limbs—KABOOM!—down he goes into the pit and I've got him!"

"How deep is it?" Bert asked.

"Seven feet," said Henry proudly.

Freddie whistled. "And you dug it all by yourself?"

"Well, not exactly all of it," said Henry, scuffling his foot. "There was a big hole here where Daddy blasted out an old tree trunk."

"Still, it was a big job," said Nan warmly.

"And it might work," added Bert, as they started for the house.

After a delicious supper of crisply fried fish, Bert and Freddie helped Uncle Walter feed the pony and the chickens. The girls wrote postcards to their parents and friends.

At dusk, Aunt Doris whistled for the children from the back porch. She invited them to drive with her to a small store in the nearby town for homemade ice cream. They called Henry several times, but he did not appear.

"Well, that's too bad," said Aunt Doris. "He'll have to stay home with Daddy."

At the store the children ordered triple scoops of thick, creamy ice cream in big cones. Nan bought a small carton of chocolate ice cream for Henry. It was nearly dark when Aunt Doris let them out near the back door of the farmhouse and drove into the garage by the barn. As Bert started up the back steps he stopped short.

"Look!" he exclaimed. "Footprints—*purple* footprints!"

CHAPTER IV

RUNAWAY SHEEP

"PURPLE footprints!" exclaimed Freddie as he and the others crowded around Bert.

In the dusk they could make out large shoe marks leading up to the screen door. Bert opened it, and as they stepped into the kitchen they saw that the prints led to the hall.

"Go quietly," he said softly. "They might belong to the prowler!"

Nan put the carton of ice cream on the table. Then, single file, the twins and Nellie followed the shoe marks to the staircase. Dark patches showed on the steps. The children tiptoed to the top. The footprints led to the door of Aunt Doris and Uncle Walter's room.

"The prowler must be in there!" Freddie whispered.

Bert quietly stepped to the door. As he put his hand on the knob, Nan grabbed his arm.

"Wait!" she whispered. "Maybe we ought to

call Uncle Walter first. It may be dangerous."

The next moment the children heard a heavy step inside. Before they could move, the door jerked open. *Uncle Walter!*

"What's going on out here?" he asked, surprised.

Quickly the children explained. "The prints lead right into your room," said Bert.

"And no wonder!" exclaimed Nan. "The purple stuff is on your feet, Uncle Walter!"

The big man looked down at his rough brown work shoes. On the edge of the sole could be seen a glob of dark stuff. He lifted up his foot and examined the bottom. There was a dark stain on it and also one on the other shoe.

"Hey! We have it too!" Freddie said. The children looked at their soles and saw that they had a few purple patches.

A board creaked on the steps below. The children looked over the railing. Henry was coming up the steps with his eyes on the purple patches.

"What are you doing?" Freddie called.

Startled, Henry glanced up. His face clouded, and he put his hands on his hips. "Did you step in my trap and make these footprints?" he asked indignantly.

"Oh, Henry! Not another trap!" came his mother's voice. Mrs. Zoop had just come into the hall.

"You mean that you made that purple stuff?"

Bert asked as the children started downstairs.

"Speak up, Henry," said his father sternly as he followed the others.

The boy looked miserable. "It would have worked fine, if everybody hadn't gone stepping on it," he said. "I took some Easter-egg dye and mixed it with water and dry earth. I made some nice purple mud. I was doing that in the cellar when you called me a while ago," he added. "Then I spread it at the foot of the back steps. I figured that if the prowler sneaked into the house his footprints would give him away."

"Henry," said his mother firmly, "this mess will have to be cleaned up tonight."

Without a word the boy walked off to the kitchen and soon returned with a brush and dustpan.

"We'll help you," said Nan. The girls went for warm soapy water and rags.

Twenty minutes later, the kitchen, hall, stairs, and bedroom were as clean as the children could make them. "Whatever is left I can take care of tomorrow," said Mrs. Zoop.

Suddenly Nan's hands flew to her mouth. "Oh Henry, your ice cream!" She led the way to the kitchen and handed the bag to Henry. "We bought this for you, but I'm afraid it's soup by now."

Henry took the bag sadly. "Well, thanks anyway. And also for helping me clean up."

The others watched as he poured his ice cream into a glass and drank it.

"Maybe you'll have better luck with your next trap," said Freddie.

"I sure hope so. I'm tired of catching you Bobbseys."

In the morning Aunt Doris drove to Lancaster, taking the twins and Nellie with her. Henry stayed home to keep an eye on his Prowler Pit.

The children watched eagerly from the car windows as they passed through rolling green farmland. Here and there were herds of black-and-white cows and large red barns with stone foundations.

Once they passed two boys pitching hay into a wagon with a mule harnessed to it.

"Look how funny they're dressed!" Flossie exclaimed. The boys wore plain blue pants with suspenders and light blue shirts. On their heads were wide-brimmed dark hats.

"They're Amish," Aunt Doris explained. "Because of their religion, they dress very plainly. They use horses and buggies instead of cars, and most of their clothes are homemade. They're called plain Dutch, while people like us are called fancy Dutch. That's because we like pretty colors and decorations. Some of the Amish people live near us," she added, "so you may meet them."

In about an hour the travelers entered the narrow, busy streets of Lancaster. Women hurried along carrying small baskets.

"We'll go to the largest market," said Aunt Doris.

She parked the car at the curb, and the children followed her up an alley to a large red brick building. The aisles were crowded with people. Rows and rows of stalls were piled high with bright-colored fruits and fresh vegetables.

"Oh, look!" exclaimed Nan, indicating a stall with huge cauliflowers in neat rows.

Freddie grinned. "They're bigger than Flossie's head."

His twin laughed. "And there's a cabbage as big as yours, Freddie!"

The children walked past counters of homemade pies and bread, and sniffed deeply. "Oh, it all smells so good!" Nan exclaimed.

"We'd better look for the Meyer cheese stall," Bert suggested.

"It's at the end of this aisle," said Aunt Doris. "You go ahead. We'll meet at the car."

The children worked their way down the aisle to it and joined a crowd around a lighted glass case. Inside were many kinds of cheese, including great chunks of holey Swiss cheese and tubs of a yellow buttery variety.

Patiently the children waited their turn. Finally a thin young man with dark hair smiled at them. "Well, what will it be?" he asked.

"We just want to ask a question," said Nan quickly. She introduced herself. "Do you know a Dr. Fox?"

"Or a Mr. Drucker?" Bert added. He then described the light-haired prowler. "Sometimes he wears a dark wig and mustache."

"I remember a blond fellow like that," said the clerk. "He was here last week and bought lots of cheese."

Nan explained that the police wanted to question the man. "Do you know where we can find him?"

"No. But try the flower stall run by the fancy Dutch woman. He went there, too."

After thanking the clerk, the children walked over to the flower stand. A smiling woman stood behind the counter. Nan questioned her about Dr. Fox, but she could not remember him.

As Nan thanked her and turned away, Nellie pointed out a sign: *Buy a four-leaf clover for luck. Twenty-five cents.* It was stuck in a low vase of the plants.

Bert said, "Those are big like the ones on the Zoops' clover bank."

For a while the children walked through the busy market hoping to catch a glimpse of Dr. Fox, but they had no luck. When they reached the farm, Henry reported that he had not caught the prowler either.

After lunch Flossie said to Aunt Doris,

"Freddie and I want to play with the sheep in the field. May we?"

"Yes," she replied, "but be sure to shut the gate when you go in and out, so none of the sheep get away. Uncle Walter won't like it if they do."

"We'll be careful," Freddie promised.

A few minutes later, the young twins opened the white picket gate, slipped inside, and shut it tight.

"Let's look for lucky clovers," said Flossie as they strolled among the woolly animals. Suddenly she stopped short beside a tree. "Here's a big clump!" she exclaimed.

"Look!" Freddie said excitedly, pulling her sleeve.

He nodded toward the woods at the top of the slope. Two children were peering over the fence. The boy was wearing a large-brimmed hat. The girl had on a long pink dress and white cap.

"They're Amish!" whispered Freddie.

"Hello!" called Flossie as she and her twin ran toward them. Instantly the boy and girl ducked back among the trees.

"Don't go!" Flossie called. "Please come back!"

"We just want to talk to you!" Freddie called.

At the top of the slope there was another gate. Flossie opened it, and the Bobbseys dashed into

"They're running away!" Freddie cried

the woods after the Amish children. But they had disappeared.

When the twins turned back, Freddie gave a cry of alarm. "They're running away!" A big sheep was coming out of the open gate, and two more were coming after it.

Frightened, the twins ran back and closed the gate. Then they tried to catch the runaways. The scared animals darted this way and that through the woods and down the back of the hill. Flossie and Freddie chased after them. Finally the children stopped, gasping, on a dirt road.

"They're gone!" said Flossie, her voice trembling. "Uncle Walter is going to be very angry."

As she spoke the twins heard thunder.

"And now it's going to rain!" said Freddie, looking worried. "But we can't go back. We must find the sheep."

As the twins followed the road, drops of rain began to fall. Some distance ahead they saw an old-fashioned covered bridge.

"Let's go there," said Freddie.

The children raced ahead with the big raindrops spattering in the dust around them. As they ran inside the gloomy bridge, their footsteps echoed hollowly on the boards.

Flossie shivered. "It's scary in here."

The next moment they heard a weird noise.

Woooo!

CHAPTER V

WOO AND BOO!

"WHAT was that?" Flossie asked fearfully.

The strange noise came again. It seemed to be high in the rafters of the covered bridge. The children looked up and saw two glowing yellow eyes in a corner.

"Woo!"

"An owl!" exclaimed Flossie. The twins giggled.

The next moment there was a loud rattling sound and two headlights pierced the gloom at the other end of the bridge.

"Hello!" called a voice. "What are you doing here?" It was Otto Hummel in his pickup truck.

He stopped beside the children, who quickly explained about the open gate.

"Get in at once," said Otto. "We'll look for the sheep."

As the twins climbed into the front seat, he

shook his head. "Such a day! It gives chust what I thought—*Donnerwetter.*"

Seeing their puzzled looks, he added, "That means thunder weather—a storm. *Donner* is thunder."

"Like Donner and Blitzen, Santa's reindeer," said Flossie.

As the truck rolled out into the daylight, Freddie asked why the Amish children had run away.

"The plain people like to keep to themselves," Otto replied, "so the youngsters are shy."

Suddenly Freddie pointed across a meadow toward a clump of trees. "Our sheep!"

"Ja," said Otto. "I recognize that big one." The artist pulled over to the side of the road. "Come on! We'll go up on 'em easy and grab 'em by the neck wool."

He swung down from the truck, and the children followed him across the meadow. The sheep were swiftly caught and loaded into the back of the truck.

The rain had stopped when Otto pulled up at the Cloverbank barn. Mr. Zoop came out to meet them. When he saw the sheep, his face grew stern. Freddie and Flossie looked shamefaced as they told him what had happened.

"We're very sorry, Uncle Walter," said Freddie. Flossie's eyes filled with tears.

"Well, there's no harm done this time," he

said quietly, "but after this you must be very careful."

The young twins helped the two men put the sheep back in their pasture. Then they thanked Otto for his help.

For a while Freddie and Flossie felt bad about what had happened, but soon they were eating a hearty supper and telling about their adventure.

"We were lucky to find the sheep," said Freddie.

"I guess the four-leaf clovers brought us luck," said Flossie and told about finding the clump under the tree.

"That's odd," said Aunt Doris. "I didn't know we had any big patches of it."

"I hope the rest of us are lucky enough to meet some Amish children," Nan put in.

While it was still light, the young detectives searched for the outside opening to the secret passage. Henry followed as they checked the earthen floor in the barn for a hidden trapdoor and examined the ground outside. Some distance away was a long, low building with no windows.

"What's that?" asked Bert.

"The wagon shed," said Henry.

As they walked around it, the twins noticed that the far side was open. The visitors stopped short in surprise.

"Look at that!" Bert exclaimed. "A covered

wagon!" He gazed at the long, rounded canvas top.

"Why didn't you tell us you had this?" Freddie asked Henry. "It's great!"

"I thought you'd seen it by now."

"We didn't," said Bert. Next to the wagon was a large, shiny red cart.

"Is this what Daisy pulls?" Freddie asked.

Henry nodded, then added proudly, "The covered wagon is a real Conestoga wagon, the kind the pioneers in our country used to cross the prairies to the West."

"We know," said Nan. "They loaded all their belongings into them—furniture, mirrors, cooking pots, food, and everything."

"Some of these were drawn by teams of oxen," Bert remarked.

"In the Farm Show, this one will be pulled by six horses," said Henry. "That's the number always used with these wagons."

"Where are the horses?" asked Flossie.

"They belong to a friend of my father's," was the reply. "They're at his place. You'll see them next week when they pull this wagon in the Show."

He explained that it was held at the local fairgrounds every year. "People show livestock and vegetables and quilts and stuff."

Freddie looked longingly at the wagon. "I sure wish we could ride in that."

Henry pointed to a big wooden canoe. "That's mine, too."

"You have some neat things," said Bert.

The young detectives went on searching for a hidden entrance to a passageway until it grew too dark to see, but found nothing.

Next morning after breakfast Aunt Doris said she had to work on her trunks. "I'm going to exhibit them in the Farm Show," she explained, and hurried out to the barn.

"The Conestoga has to be ready, too," said Uncle Walter. "You boys want to help fix it up?"

The three eagerly agreed and trooped off with him. Meanwhile the girls made the beds.

As Nellie was fluffing Henry's pillow, she glanced out the window and saw a small, skinny man with a battered suitcase slip into the backyard. He was wearing a baggy brown suit, much too big for him.

"Come here, quick!" Nellie said to the others. Nan and Flossie hurried over.

They saw the man stop by Sheela's pen and glance nervously over his shoulder. Then he smoothed down his thin red hair.

"He acts kind of sneaky," said Flossie.

The older girls agreed, and the three went quickly downstairs. As they entered the kitchen they saw the man peering through the screen door.

"May we help you?" Nellie said politely. The fellow looked startled and stood up straight.

"I just wondered if you wanted to buy some needles and pins," he said. "I'm a peddler."

As he spoke, his bright brown eyes darted around the kitchen, seeming to take in everything. Nan quietly hooked the screen door.

"I don't think we want any," said Nellie.

"Oh, come on now," said the man, pulling on the door handle. "Let me come in. It will only take a minute."

"No, thank you," Nellie said politely.

The man smiled, showing a crooked front tooth. "Are you young ladies home alone?" he asked.

"No, we're not," said Nan quickly. "Flossie, run and tell Aunt Doris a peddler is here."

Without a word the little girl ran out the front way and raced around to the barn. As soon as she left, the man scowled.

"Never mind! I haven't got time to wait around!"

Taking his bag, he hastened off the porch. He skirted past a large mud puddle at the foot of the steps, then disappeared around the corner. A minute later the girls heard the roar of a car motor.

"He's gone," said Nellie. "Let's go meet Aunt Doris."

As the girls started down the porch steps, a

beat-up old car shot into the backyard with the peddler at the wheel. He drove right through the big puddle.

SPLAT!

The girls screeched and jumped back as the muddy water splashed them. The man laughed, made a wide turn, and roared off.

Aunt Doris came hurrying over with Flossie. The girls told her what had happened.

"That was Skinny Broome," she said, frowning. She explained that every summer the peddler came to this area. "He has been caught stealing things at several farms," she went on, "and if people won't buy from him, he does damage."

"He's bad," said Flossie, as the older girls went upstairs to change to fresh shorts. "I hope he doesn't come back."

After lunch the Bobbseys and Nellie invited Henry to go with them to the cellar to search for the secret passage.

"Not me," he replied. "I've looked there already."

Taking flashlights, the visitors hurried to the kitchen. At the top of the cellar stairs they turned on the light. Bert led the way down into the laundry room. After searching carefully and examining the tubs and the walls, they moved into the next room. Bert found the wall switch. A dim light went on, showing a huge gray fur-

SPLAT!

nace. Suddenly they heard a soft clinking sound.

"What was that?" Nan asked.

Clink-clink.

"It's coming from behind the furnace," Freddie whispered.

The detectives edged forward quietly. As they did, the noise moved farther away. Rounding the furnace, they saw a doorway into a dark passage. The noise was coming from there!

Bert could find no light switch. He turned on his flash and stepped into the little corridor, with the others close behind.

Clink!

Silently Bert pointed to a closet door which was ajar. As he reached for the handle, the door swung open.

"BOO!"

The girls screamed and Bert jumped back.

"Henry!" cried Nan.

"I scared you that time," the boy said, grinning. He held up a jelly glass and a knife and clinked them together.

"Henry Zoop!" exclaimed his cousin. "You're not funny!"

Henry chuckled. "If you're such great detectives, how come you were so scared?" He walked away, whistling.

For the next hour the children searched for the secret passage but found nothing. After supper Henry went off by himself, while Nellie and the young twins watched television.

Bert and Nan took a walk up to the sheep meadow. At the top of the slope they looked over the fence, hoping to see some Amish children. But none came. As it grew darker the birds twittered sleepily.

"We'd better go back," said Bert.

On the way Nan stopped under the tree to pick a four-leaf clover. She noticed that the whole patch was setting loosely in the ground. "That's funny," she thought. "It looks as if somebody tried to dig it up. Who would want to steal a bunch of lucky clover?"

Just then Bert called softly from the bottom of the hill, "Nan! Come here quick!" She hurried down to him.

"Look!" he whispered and pointed behind the barn to the Prowler Pit. Most of the boughs which had lain across the top were gone. The few remaining ones were shaking. There was something in Henry's trap!

"We'd better take a look!" said Bert softly.

CHAPTER VI

A DANGEROUS SPY

THE children approached the pit cautiously. Branches covering it went on moving. Bert leaned over and peered down into the trap.

"Henry!" he exclaimed.

The trapped boy stopped struggling to get out. He looked up, red-faced.

"Are you hurt?" Bert asked him.

"No."

"How did you ever get in there?" Nan said.

"I fell in, of course, silly," said Henry angrily.

"Why didn't you call for help?" Bert questioned.

"'Cause I knew everybody would laugh at me." The twins tried not to smile.

"We'll get you out," said Bert, reaching down a hand. Nan grabbed Henry's other hand. He managed to scramble out of the hole.

Brushing the dirt and leaves off his clothes,

Henry explained that he had been hiding just inside the barn door to watch for the prowler.

"Suddenly there was a noise outside. It was coming from back here. As I ran around the corner, I forgot about the pit."

"What was the noise?" asked Bert.

"A deer," said Henry glumly. "I saw it bound into the woods just as I was falling. Are you going to tell everybody?" he added anxiously.

"Not if you don't want us to," said Nan.

"Well, I don't," Henry answered. "I feel silly."

"You shouldn't," said Bert. "If you had been the prowler, the whole case might have been solved by now."

"Yes," said Nan quickly. "You have great ideas." Henry looked pleased.

"We ought to work together," said Bert earnestly. "Then Dr. Fox wouldn't have a chance. Come on! How about it?"

Henry looked at their eager faces. "Okay," he said.

"We'd better work fast," said Nan. "If Dr. Fox finds that golden gift before we do, he'll steal it. I *wish* we had a clue to the secret passageway."

"I think there's an entrance to it somewhere along the bank of the creek," said Henry. "You know it was built in case of Indian attack. Well, if the war party circled the house and the barn, the family would need a tunnel which came out somewhere behind the Indians."

"That's right," Bert agreed.

"But I've already looked and looked," Henry told him.

"Let's search together tomorrow," Nan suggested.

As the boys agreed, they heard the loud crack of a twig. Startled, the children looked toward the woods, but saw nothing.

"It was probably a deer again," said Henry.

Back in the house, the detectives found everyone watching television. Nan told about their plans for the next morning. "Henry has decided to work with us," she added.

"That's cool!" exclaimed Freddie as Flossie and Nellie agreed. "Now that old prowler better watch out!"

Aunt Doris wished them luck. "But the day after tomorrow you must keep free," she went on. "We are going to a barn-raising."

Henry's eyebrows shot up and he exclaimed, "That's keen! Whose barn—Gruber's?"

"Yes."

Henry explained that if an Amish farmer's barn was destroyed by fire, all the neighboring plain people would come and help him put up a new one. "A barn-raising's great," said Henry, " 'cause it's like a big party with lots of food."

"But you aren't Amish," said Nellie.

"I know," said Aunt Doris, "but we are friendly with the Grubers and want to help them. Everybody is welcome." She smiled. "There's lots to do. I'll be up long before daylight baking pies and cakes."

"Oh, may we help?" Flossie asked.

Aunt Doris laughed. "If you're not a sleepyhead!"

The next morning shortly after breakfast the six children headed into the woods behind the barn to start their search. Henry and Bert had found a couple of old broom handles in the wagon shed. The girls had rakes, and the young twins carried stout sticks.

When they reached the bank of the stream, Bert said, "How about three of us working on one side and three on the other?"

The others agreed. They moved slowly downhill along the banks, raking and probing with their tools. Now and then they all worked together to roll aside a large stone. But there was no sign of a hole in the ground.

At the bottom they stood on the wooded shore and watched the creek bubble into a small river.

"No use going any farther," said Bert, wiping his face with his sleeve. "I don't think the tunnel could come this far from the house. It would be too hard to build."

"That's right," said Henry.

"I'm tired of detecting," said Freddie, flopping down on the ground.

"So am I," Flossie added. "Let's go back and play with Sheela."

"Go ahead," said Nan.

As the young twins started slowly up the hill, she turned to the others. "What shall we do now?"

"I wish we could find where Dr. Fox is staying," said Bert. "Since the police haven't picked him up in a motel or a rooming house, maybe he's camping out some place."

"I know!" Henry exclaimed. "Let's take my canoe and see if we can spot a camp. I know a place a couple of miles from here where we can have a cookout. It belongs to Farmer Cooper, and he gave me permission to picnic there."

An hour later the four children were skimming down the river. Bert and Henry paddled while Nan and Nellie sat in the middle with the picnic basket at their feet.

"This is fun!" exclaimed Nan as the breeze ruffled her hair.

Nellie trailed her hand in the cool, sparkling water. All of them watched the shores carefully for a camp.

Before long they passed beneath a small bridge. A little later the canoe glided under the big covered one. There was no sign of anyone living on the banks. Gradually the stream grew narrower and deeper.

"There are rapids ahead and a falls," said Henry.

"A falls!" exclaimed Nellie. "We don't want to be swept over it. Let's stop here!"

"It's way ahead," said Henry easily. "And anyhow, this is just a low falls. Not much higher than a tall man."

"Even so," said Nan, "It would be dangerous to go over it."

Ten minutes later they came to a low, wide clearing on the bank. In the middle was a stone fireplace. "That's Cooper's place," Henry said.

The boys steered the canoe to shore and pulled it up on the sandy bank near some bushes.

"We'll unpack the lunch," Nan said, "and you boys get wood for the fire."

Bert and Henry hurried into the woods, and the girls carried the basket to the fireplace. As they were taking out frankfurters and rolls, they heard a scraping noise.

"Look!" Nan gasped. She pointed toward the bushes.

A man's foot was sticking out of the brush and pushing their canoe into the water!

"This'll teach you kids to mind your own business!" came a rough voice. *Dr. Fox?*

"You stop that!" cried Nan angrily.

As Nellie ran for the boys, Nan raced toward the canoe.

But it had floated free. Though she waded in after it, the current caught the craft and drew it farther away. Nan began to swim out.

Faster and faster the canoe went. She could not catch it.

Suddenly she remembered the falls! Nan tried to swim to shore, but the current was too strong. "Help!" she called.

The next moment she was tumbled into the rapids. Nan grasped wildly at rocks, trying to hang on, but they were too round and slippery. Straight ahead was the drop-off!

Meanwhile Bert and Henry heard her cry and came out of the woods on a run.

"Save her! Save her!" Nellie cried.

"We'll make better time along the shore," said Bert. "Come on!"

The three raced down the bank of the stream.

"I'll go out for her as soon as I'm closer!" called Bert, who outdistanced Nellie and Henry.

Moments later the canoe went over the falls.

"Help!" screamed Nan, as she was swept over the edge after it.

Bert tore down the steep slope beside the cascade. At the bottom he saw the canoe wedged upside down between two rocks. Nan was clinging to it.

"Help!" Nan called

"Hang on!" Bert cried. "I'm coming!"

He plunged into the river and swam to his twin. Nellie and Henry followed. Together the three dragged Nan and the canoe to shore.

"Are you all right?" Bert asked his twin.

"Y-yes. And thanks, kids."

Henry looked over the canoe and decided it was undamaged. "Dr. Fox sure is trying to scare us off!" he declared.

"I'll bet he made that noise in the woods last night," said Bert. "He was eavesdropping."

"Yes, and he probably was spying this morning and followed us here," said Nan.

"I guess he heard me say we were going to Cooper's," Henry remarked. "All he had to do was drive to the farm, walk through the woods to the picnic spot and wait for us."

Nellie shivered. "We're all soaked, but I guess the sun will dry our clothes." By the time the four had carried the canoe back to the cook-out place, they felt warm again.

"We may as well eat," said Bert.

In a few minutes the frankfurters were sizzling on the grill and four pairs of sandals were drying around the edge of the fire. The hungry detectives finished the meal with chocolate cake, fruit, and a large Thermos of milk.

After tidying the picnic spot, the children put out the fire and piled up some wood for the next picnickers. Then they started for home in the canoe. The boys had been paddling about ten minutes when Henry looked down and gasped.

"Water! There's a leak!"

"Head for shore!" Bert exclaimed.

His sister snatched up the picnic basket and put it next to her on the seat. Then, using their hands, Nan and Nellie tried to bail out the water. But it flowed in faster and faster.

"We're sinking!" cried Nan.

CHAPTER VII

THE MISSING RING

THE two girls worked frantically to scoop the water out of the canoe, while Bert and Henry paddled hard for shore. In a few minutes the bow hit the grassy bank. The children leaped out and pulled the craft onto land.

The boys examined the hole in the bottom of the canoe. "This must have happened when it went over the falls," said Henry gloomily.

Nellie sighed. "I guess it means we'll have to walk home."

Henry nodded.

"But what will we do with the canoe?" Nan asked. "It's too heavy to carry so far."

"And we can't leave it here. Somebody might take it," Nellie added.

Some distance away through the trees they could see the rear of a white frame house with a fence around it.

"Maybe those people would let us leave it in

their yard," Nan suggested. "Then Uncle Walter could come for it tonight in the station wagon."

Bert carried the picnic basket as the four children put the canoe on their shoulders and started toward the house.

As they neared it, they saw a dozen new rocking chairs lined up in the yard. Bright-colored tulips and *distelfinks* were painted on the backs.

"Oh, aren't they pretty!" Nellie exclaimed.

Nan sniffed the air. "They've just been varnished. Smell them?"

Bert opened the gate and the children filed in. A slender young man in dark trousers and white shirt stepped out of the house. He wore a blue cap and had on rimless glasses. With a little smile he walked over to them. His mild brown eyes were friendly, but he said nothing. Bert explained what had happened, and asked permission to leave the canoe.

The young man nodded. "Be *donkbawr* you weren't hurt," he said as the children put the craft down.

The visitors looked puzzled and Henry explained that *donkbawr* meant thankful.

The man examined the broken place in the canoe. "I'll fix it," he said, and went into the house. Soon he came back carrying a hammer, some nails and a piece of plywood. A sign in the window read: *Carl Fenster, Chairs.*

"Are you Mr. Fenster?" she asked as the young man stooped down beside the canoe and began to work.

He looked up, smiled slightly, and nodded. Nan introduced herself and the others.

"They're all staying with us," put in Henry. "I live at Cloverbank Farm."

Carl stopped hammering. "I heard something about your farm the other day."

"What was it?" Henry asked.

"Did you know Cloverbank used to have a special hex sign of its own? It was not like any of the usual designs."

"No," said Henry, surprised.

Nan looked interested. "What was it like?"

The chairmaker shook his head. "I don't know. No one does, really, except that it had a four-leaf clover in the center."

"Where did you hear about it?" Bert asked.

Mr. Fenster explained that the day before, he had gone to a birthday party for his uncle, who was a very old man.

"Someone mentioned hex signs, and Uncle told about the one which used to be on the Cloverbank barn. He never saw it. But he had heard about it as a child. David Scott, the last of that family, made the sign himself and fastened it to the barn. He didn't paint the hex on as most folks do. Just before he sold the farm to the Hummels, the barn burned down."

"The sign was probably destroyed in the fire," said Nellie.

"Maybe," the young man replied quietly, "but my uncle says the barn was hit by lightning. Sometimes when that happens the iron nails will fall out. If they did, the sign could have dropped off."

"Was the new barn built on the foundation of the old one?" Bert asked.

Mr. Fenster nodded.

"Maybe the sign is still around," said Bert. "It could be lying somewhere near the barn, but of course it would be covered with earth and brush after so many years."

"I don't think you could find it now any more," said the chairmaker.

"Perhaps someone picked it up after the fire and saved the sign," Nan suggested.

"Then it could be anywhere," said Mr. Fenster, "—maybe in somebody's attic."

In a few minutes he had finished nailing a patch on the bottom of the canoe. The children thanked him and offered to pay for the repair, but he shook his head, smiling. "Just get home safe."

On the way to the river, Nan said, "Maybe the hex sign was made different from the others, because it tells something special about Cloverbank Farm."

"That's what I was thinking too!" Bert

agreed. "Maybe it gives a clue to the secret passage."

"That's an idea!" said Henry. "Now all we have to do is find the sign!" His face fell. "We haven't one chance in a thousand."

"We must try anyhow," Nellie said firmly.

It was mid-afternoon when the four reached home and reported what had happened. Then all six children searched around the barn, hoping they might unearth the old hex sign. But by suppertime they had found nothing. While they were eating, Aunt Doris reminded them that the next day was the barn-raising.

"That means everybody up early!" said Uncle Walter with a grin. "And I mean before the birds!"

It was just beginning to get light when the children's alarm clocks woke them. Quickly they dressed and hurried down to the kitchen. Aunt Doris was already there setting out bowls and pans. She had taken off her gold wedding ring and put it on the window sill over the sink.

After breakfast, the boys helped Uncle Walter with the chores. Aunt Doris gave each girl a large apron, and they began to work.

"Flossie," she said, "would you please bring in the dish towels I have drying on the porch?"

As Flossie opened the screen door, the blue jay flew into the kitchen.

"No, no!" cried Flossie, "Go on out, Jiffy!"

"Let him alone now," said Aunt Doris. "We have no time to waste. He'll sit on his perch."

The bird settled down on a curtain rod and watched the baking with his beady black eyes. Later, as Flossie was sifting flour, she glanced up and gave a cry.

"No, no, Jiffy, drop it!" she cried and darted toward the bird.

He had the gold ring in his beak! He dropped it and she picked up the ring.

"Put it on the table here," said Aunt Doris, who was beating the batter in a big bowl. As Flossie obeyed, Aunt Doris wiped her hands on her apron. "Now we must get the *schnitz,*" she said.

"What's a *schnitz?*" asked Nellie, giggling.

"Dried apples," her aunt replied. She moved two fingers like a scissors. "*Schnitz* in Pennsylvania German means to cut. Every year we slice up lots of apples and let them dry. Then we use them in our cooking. Come along."

She led the way to a cold cellar in the basement. On its shelves were many large trays of dried apples covered with clean dish towels. Each girl took one of the trays upstairs.

Aunt Doris poured batter into the baking pans. Then the girls arranged the apples in neat circles on top.

"Ten cakes!" exclaimed Flossie. "Um yum."

Soon the air was filled with the sweet, spicy

smell of baking cakes. Aunt Doris now looked for her ring but could not find the wedding band.

"Where did it go?" Nellie asked.

Flossie glanced up at the blue jay on his curtain rod. "Jiffy, did you take it?"

The bird cocked his head.

"You know, we were all down the cellar for a while," Nellie said thoughtfully. "What if Dr. Fox came in and took the ring?"

"Yes, or Skinny Broome," Nan added.

Aunt Doris gave a sigh. Tears filled her eyes. "My wedding ring means a lot to me."

Nellie patted her aunt's hand. "I'm sure it will turn up. We'll all keep looking for it."

By eight o'clock the warm cakes were packed in a big basket which the boys put in the back of the station wagon. Then everybody got in and Uncle Walter drove to the Gruber farm.

The first thing they saw was a large stone foundation with a huge wooden framework above it. Men were already on ladders raising boards into place for a new barn.

Under the trees next to the farmhouse stood long wooden tables where Amish women were unpacking baskets of food. The girls and Aunt Doris carried their cakes over to them.

Meanwhile the boys went to the partly finished barn with Uncle Walter. Mr. Gruber, a stocky man with a black beard and wide-

The bird had the ring in his beak!

brimmed black hat, welcomed them warmly.

"I'm *donkbawr* to have such good help," he said, smiling at the boys. "Come with me once."

While Uncle Walter joined the carpenters, Mr. Gruber took the boys to the other end of the building. He suggested they carry boards to the men who would nail them into place.

As the sun became hotter Freddie pulled a cap from his pocket and put it on. But soon his head felt too hot. He pulled off the cap and laid it down, then wandered off to look at the food.

At noon the women called the men to come and eat. As they walked toward the shady grove, Henry tapped Freddie on the shoulder and pointed to the topmost beam of the barn. There was Freddie's cap! Some of the men had turned to watch him, and now they laughed.

"That's a regular barn-raising joke," Henry explained, grinning, "to nail somebody's hat to a beam!"

As the carpenters hurried off to eat, Freddie eyed a tall ladder resting against the barn.

"I'll show them! I'll get it!" he thought.

Quickly he ran over and began to climb. At the top he looked down. His heart sank! He was very high above the earth!

Carefully he crept onto the wide beam toward his cap. He grasped the cap and found it was not nailed fast. Then he began to inch his way downward. Suddenly his foot hit the ladder.

He heard yells from below and a voice cried, "Watch out! The ladder's falling!" The next moment there was a loud crash.

Freddie clung tightly to the rafters. He was frightened. High in the air, how was he going to get down?

CHAPTER VIII

A WILD RACE

"HELP! I'm stuck!" cried Freddie.

"Hold on!" came Bert's voice from below. "We'll get you down!"

Freddie hugged the beam and shut his eyes so he would not see the ground far below. Soon he heard a thud as the ladder was placed against the barn again. A few minutes later Uncle Walter's head appeared.

"Okay, son. Easy now."

Firm hands gripped Freddie's legs as the man helped him backward onto the ladder. Uncle Walter kept hold of Freddie, as the two crept down. At the bottom several of the men were waiting anxiously with Mr. Gruber.

"Well, we played a joke on you," the farmer said to the little boy, "and you gave us a bad scare, so I guess we're even."

Holding his cap, Freddie looked sheepish and said he was sorry.

"Never mind," said Mr. Gruber, "let's go eat ourselves full."

In a few minutes everyone was seated at the long tables, eating hungrily. There was plenty of fried chicken and potato salad, sweet pickles and home-baked rolls.

When they reached dessert, Nan suddenly had an idea. "Aunt Doris!" she exclaimed. "Maybe your ring is in one of the cakes!"

Mrs. Zoop looked surprised. Then, seeing that the others at the table were puzzled, she explained what had happened.

"Why do you think the ring is in the cake?" Nellie asked Nan.

"I'll bet Jiffy Jay tried to pick it up again while we were in the cellar, and maybe he dropped it!"

"Right in the batter!" exclaimed Nellie. "Oh, Aunt Doris, be careful when you cut the cakes! Maybe you'll find it!"

"And everybody be careful when you eat your piece," said Nan.

Aunt Doris had spread the ten cakes across one end of the table. Now she took a large knife from her basket. "Here Nan," she said, smiling. "You cut them."

While everyone watched eagerly, Nan began to cut the first slice. Suddenly, in the third one, the knife hit something.

Nan gasped. "I think I've found it!"

Carefully she lifted the slice of apple cake out of the pan and put it on a plate. Gleaming in the side of it was a bit of gold!

"Oh, there it is!" Flossie cried.

Nan took a fork and deftly picked out the gold ring. She handed it to Mrs. Zoop. As the people at the table applauded, Aunt Doris kissed Nan.

"You're a dear, clever girl!" She polished the ring lovingly and slipped it on her finger. "I just can't tell you how glad I am to have it back."

As Nan beamed, Otto Hummel spoke up. "Such a good detective!"

Ten minutes later Nan drew him aside and told him about the special hex sign for Cloverbank Farm.

He looked surprised. "That is a wonder. I didn't know there was such a sign." His eyes sparkled. "I would like to have this hex. Would you children try to find that old sign?"

"We'd love to," said Nan. She explained that they hoped it would be a clue to the secret passageway. "Have you any idea where to look?"

"The sign might turn up in a country auction," he said. "Every once in a while somebody sells his farm and house with everything in. You ought to go to a couple of auctions. It would be fun anyhow."

Nan went over to the other children and told them about the newest job for them. Then

Henry suggested that they walk to the neighboring farm to see the six horses which would be used to pull the Conestoga wagon.

They started off across the fields. Flossie looked back at a table where the Amish children were seated with their parents.

"They're so shy," she remarked. "I saw the boy and girl who were watching us at Cloverbank, but they didn't want to talk to me."

"Some of them say a few words, then run away," Freddie added.

Ten minutes later the children passed a grove of maple trees and went through a wide wooden gate into the next property. Henry led them past the farmhouse.

"This family's over at the barn-raising now," he said, "but Daddy's friend said the hired man would show us the horses."

He led them behind the barn to a corral. There stood six beautiful white horses!

"Hi, Henry!" called a small man with sandy hair and beard. He was taking hay from a nearby bale.

"Hi, Luke!" said Henry. He introduced the others. "May we help you?"

"Sure," Luke said. "Throw the horses over the fence some hay."

The older children managed not to smile at the funny Pennsylvania Dutch expression, but Flossie and Freddie had to giggle.

While the children were tossing hay into the corral, Luke added, "I'm *donkbawr* you came because I can leave now. I have to go to Lebanon up."

He said good-by and walked off quickly.

After throwing the hay in, the children sat on the corral fence and watched the animals.

"They're really big and strong!" Bert exclaimed.

"Yes, they have to be to pull that heavy wagon," said Henry.

"How come they call it a stogey wagon?" Flossie asked.

"Not stogey. Conestoga," said Nan. "I don't know. Where did they get the name, Henry?"

"From Conestoga, Pennsylvania. The covered wagons were first made there around 1825. That was before there were any railroads, of course. Freight was carried in 'em sometimes. They were also called prairie schooners."

"Why?" Freddie asked.

" 'Cause they could float."

As the others looked surprised, Henry explained that the wagons were built with deep wooden bottoms and could be taken off the wheels. "That was so they could go across rivers the same as boats," he explained.

"I didn't know that," said Bert, "but I read how they had wide metal wheels so they wouldn't sink in the mud."

"That's right," said Henry.

"Have you lived in this part of Pennsylvania for a long time?" Nan asked him.

"Sure. Our old farm was over by Bird-in-Hand." He grinned. "That's a town near here."

Flossie giggled. "What a funny name!"

Freddie stroked the soft nose of one of the horses. "I wish I could ride on you some time," he said.

After a while the twins and their friends started back to the barn-raising. When they passed the grove of maples, the air was filled with wild screeching. Ten or fifteen Amish children burst from the trees, yelling wildly!

"Watch out!" cried Freddie, but the next moment he went down in a heap, and the crowd of children bumped him aside and dashed on.

Bert, Henry and Nan jumped out of the way but Nellie and Flossie were knocked to the ground. As the Amish children tore across the field, Nan helped Flossie up.

"Are you hurt?" she asked.

"I'm all right," said Flossie, trying to smooth her dress.

"Well!" Nellie said and drew a deep breath. "What in the world are they doing?"

"Racing," said Henry. "The Amish kids get pretty wild sometimes when they play."

Nan giggled. "We've been wanting to meet some Amish children. Well, we certainly did!"

The young detectives walked back to the picnic tables where a stout Amish lady shook her head at Flossie. "Little girl, your dress is all *roontzeled*."

"That means it's wrinkled," said Henry.

"I couldn't help it," said Flossie to the woman. "I'm *donkbawr* it isn't torn."

The children strolled over to watch the barn being built. The huge building grew like magic. By sundown all the boards were in place. When the roof was finished a cheer went up.

Mr. Gruber thanked everyone. Then the helpers packed up their tools and started to leave in buggies and cars. By the time the Bobbsey party reached home, it was almost dark.

"It's been a long day," said Aunt Doris. "We'd better have supper and go to bed."

Soon everyone was asleep except Bert. He lay awake thinking about the prowler, thc secret passage, and the old hex sign. Restless, he got up and looked out the window.

Suddenly he became excited. Inside the pasture was a figure dressed all in black with a wide-brimmed hat. He was leaning against the fence. "Is he the prowler?" Bert thought.

Quietly Bert slipped to the next room and peeked into the girls' room. Flossie and Nellie were sound asleep.

"Nan?" he called softly.

"Yes?" his twin answered at once. She got out

"Is he the prowler?" Bert thought

of bed quickly, put on her slippers and robe and came out into the hall. "Can't you sleep either?" she whispered.

"Come here," he said. "I want to show you something." He led her to the window of his room and pointed to the slope. The figure was still there with his back to them.

Nan gasped. "What should we do? Do you think he's the prowler?"

"I don't know," her brother whispered. "I can't figure it out. He hasn't moved. What is he waiting for?"

Nan stared at the man for a few moments, then shivered. "It's kind of scary."

Bert pulled her sleeve and she followed him quietly down the hall.

"Should we call Uncle Walter?" Nan asked.

"Yes, but not right away," Bert replied. "It looks to me as if the fellow's waiting for someone. Let's sneak down and watch. As soon as the other person comes, you can run up and tell Uncle Walter. Maybe I can slip up on them and hear their conversation."

Nan and Bert crept downstairs and went outside. From the shadow of the big tree, they watched the man.

"Why doesn't he move?" Nan asked quietly. "It's creepy!"

CHAPTER IX

LUCKY DETECTIVES

THE moon went behind a cloud.

"Let's go closer," said Bert.

He and Nan ran quickly to the shelter of a small tree nearer the fence. They stared at the man, but still he did not move. Suddenly the moon came out again. The children gasped.

"It's a dummy!" Bert exclaimed. The twins hurried into the sheep meadow to examine the figure more closely.

"There's a sign on his chest," Nan remarked.

A sheet of paper was pinned to the black coat. On it was the message:

Second warning! Don't be dummies! Mind your own business!

"This must be Dr. Fox's work," said Bert grimly.

Curious, the twins examined the strange figure. It had two broomsticks for legs, a sack of wheat for a body and a cabbage for a head.

"It's a clever trick," said Bert, "but Fox is wrong if he thinks it will scare us off the case."

In the morning the older twins showed the dummy to the rest of the family. Uncle Walter said he would ride into town to report the matter to the police and also take the black clothes.

"They may have been stolen from one of our Amish neighbors."

While the children were helping Uncle Walter take the dummy apart, Freddie noticed the patch of four-leaf clovers by the fence. It was sticking up partly out of the ground. Carefully Freddie tapped it down with his toe.

"I wonder how it got loose," he said to himself.

The next moment Aunt Doris called them all to breakfast. Nan asked her how they could find out when there was to be a country auction. "Maybe we can pick up a lead there to the old Cloverbank hex."

"You could go to an auction this morning," she said. "The Hicker farm is being sold. Take the pony cart down the highway and turn off onto the dirt road. It winds back to the covered bridge. Hicker's place is just beyond it."

Eagerly the children agreed. The girls packed a lunch, while Bert helped Henry harness Daisy to the cart. Then they all climbed in. Henry took the reins and said, "Giddap."

As the pony clip-clopped briskly along the

dirt road, the children talked happily about what they would buy at the auction.

"Maybe there will be an old doll," said Flossie, clutching her little pocketbook.

Twenty minutes later, the cart turned into a wide drive. Henry stopped among the automobiles and buggies in the side yard of the farm.

The children got out and walked over to the crowd of people gathered in front of the gray frame house. The long porch was full of furniture, china, clocks, and many odds and ends.

Fascinated, the Bobbseys and their friends listened as the auctioneer, a tall, thin, bald man, offered each item for sale. He would always end with, "Going once! Going twice! Gone!"

Among the articles Nan spotted a large old-fashioned trunk with a rounded top. She and Nellie walked over to look closer.

"There's a four-leaf clover on it!" Nan exclaimed. She pointed to a faded stencil which appeared on the lid.

"Maybe it belonged to Cloverbank Farm at one time!" Nellie guessed. "Remember what Miss Lulu told us? Some families used to decorate their furniture with their own special hex."

Nan's eyes sparkled with excitement. "Let's see if we can buy this trunk for Aunt Doris. Wouldn't it be a nice gift?"

Nellie agreed. When the auctioneer finally

got to the trunk the girls made a small bid. No one else was interested.

"Sold to the two young ladies in the front row!" cried the auctioneer.

Moments later Bert and Henry hurried up to claim it. Flossie and Freddie went with them as the boys carried the trunk to the pony cart for Nan.

"Why did you buy this?" Freddie asked.

Nan explained, and Bert's eyes lit up. "This might have a clue in it to the secret passage. We'd better check it later," Nan said.

Flossie traced her plump finger over the faded design on the lid. "Another four-leaf clover," she said, "like the ones in the sheep meadow."

"There's something odd about the patch under the tree," said Nan. "I think someone tried to dig it up. It was loose in the ground."

"So was the clump by the fence!" Freddie exclaimed.

Bert frowned. "It doesn't make sense. Who would bother to steal lucky clover?"

Nellie smiled. "Now we have another puzzle!"

Flossie tugged Nan's sleeve. "There's a table of old toys at the side of the house. Let's go buy something."

The girls went with Flossie, and the boys followed a crowd of men to the barn. While Bert and Henry watched the auctioneer sell a tractor, Freddie climbed into an old sleigh.

"Jingle, jingle, jingle!" he cried. "Here we go over the snow!"

After playing awhile, he stepped across to an Amish family buggy with gray canvas sides. Freddie climbed into it and was surprised to see a man in the back seat, bending toward the floor. As he straightened up, Freddie gasped.

Dr. Fox!

The blond man stared at Freddie, then said fiercely, "Get away from here! You hear me, little boy?"

Frightened, Freddie hopped down from the buggy and raced over to Bert and Henry.

"The bad man!" Freddie exclaimed. "He's over there!"

Bert and Henry whirled just in time to see Fox hurry from the barn.

"Stop him!" Bert cried, racing after the prowler. "Catch that man!" he called to the onlookers.

But the few people who turned around were too surprised to do anything. A moment later Fox leaped into a black sedan and roared off.

Just then the auctioneer came out of the barn and Bert ran to him. "Did you see that blond man?" he asked. "Do you know who he is?"

"Sure. That's Mr. Fox, an antique dealer. For the past month he's been to most of the auctions in this area. I've worked at them all, so I know."

"He's been prowling around our farm," Henry put in. "The police are looking for him."

"Where does he live?" Freddie asked.

The auctioneer shrugged. "I never saw him before this summer."

The boys thanked the man and went to join the girls, who were waiting at the pony cart.

"Look what I bought," said Flossie happily. She opened a box with three tiny china dolls fitted snugly into it.

"That's nothing! We nearly caught Fox," said Freddie importantly. The boys reported what had happened.

Nan shook her head, puzzled. "Fox told Otto he was a writer, and he told the auctioneer he's an antique dealer. I wonder what he really is!"

"A bad, bad man," said Flossie.

The children climbed into the cart and started toward Cloverbank Farm. On the other side of the covered bridge Henry pulled off under a large tree.

"This is a good spot for lunch," he announced.

After they had eaten, Bert said he would like to examine the trunk.

"There's nothing in it," replied his twin. "Nellie and I have already looked."

"But maybe there's a false bottom with a treasure underneath," Bert said with a grin. "Let's check it over."

The girls laughed, but agreed to search. They helped the boys take the trunk from the back of the pony cart and set it down under the tree. Nan lifted the big rounded lid. The inside was lined with faded wallpaper.

"The lid is not arched inside," Bert remarked. "It's level." He tapped lightly on the flat top piece. "Maybe this comes out." With his pocket-knife he dug carefully around the edge of the lid.

"It's loosening!" he exclaimed.

The next moment the flat piece fell out and an object wrapped in faded blue cloth dropped to the bottom of the trunk.

"There *was* something in it!" Henry exclaimed. "Let's see!"

Nan had already scooped up the article. Carefully she unwound the material and laid it aside. In her hand was a round, partially burned piece of dark wood.

"It's just an old wheel or something," said Flossie, disappointed. "And it's all dirty."

But Nan's heart was pounding with excitement. "That's soot," she said, rubbing her finger on it. She turned the object over and peered closely. In the center she could make out a four-leaf clover.

"It's the Cloverbank hex sign!" Nan exclaimed.

"Let's see!" said Bert eagerly. He took the

"It's the Cloverbank hex sign!" Nan exclaimed

wood from her and looked it over. "You're right!"

Amazed, each of the children examined the discovery.

"I just can't believe it!" said Nellie. "What marvelous luck!"

"That's because of all the four-leaf clovers we found," said Flossie.

"I never thought we'd find this the first time we tried," said Nan.

"I never thought we'd find it at all," Bert added, grinning.

Freddie cried out, "Maybe it's a clue to the secret passage!"

"Give it to me," said Henry eagerly. "I'll wash it in the stream."

"No, no!" said Nan. "That sign is very old and delicate. We'd better give it to Otto. He'll know how to clean it the right way."

Bert agreed, and Nan carefully wrapped the wood in the cloth again. Half an hour later she placed it in Otto's hands.

"I cannot believe it!" he said softly, staring at the old hex. "You children are certainly remarkable."

"We were lucky," said Nan.

"I guess somebody in the Scott family picked up the sign after the fire and didn't have the heart to throw it away," said Bert, "so he put the hex in the trunk."

"Yes," Otto agreed. "Then, no doubt, it was auctioned off when the farm was sold to my family." He fingered the scorched piece of wood gingerly. "Let's take it in the sunlight once and have a good look at it."

"Do you think you can fix it?" Flossie asked anxiously as they followed him outside.

Otto's bushy brows drew down, and he squinted carefully at the antique. "Well, I can get the soot off all right. Once I see what the design is I can replace the part that's been burned away. Let me get a soft rag and I'll start."

He placed the scorched wood down carefully on the table beside the door next to a bright new hex sign. The children followed him into the barn. A few minutes later they all came out again.

Both hex signs were gone!

CHAPTER X

DONNERWETTER!

"BOTH hex signs have been stolen!" Nan cried out.

"Look! There goes Skinny Broome!" Bert exclaimed and pointed to the bottom of the hill.

The red-haired peddler jumped into his beat-up car with the two signs under his arm and roared off down the highway.

"Quick, Otto!" said Bert. "Get your truck! Maybe we can catch him!"

"I can't!" Otto replied. "I lent the truck to a friend." As they looked after the speeding car it turned onto a side road.

"Now we've got him!" exclaimed Henry. "He's heading up the lane to the little bridge."

"That's right! You've still got a chance!" said Otto. "Take the pony cart and ride down the hill behind the barn."

"That'll bring us out on River Road," Henry

put in excitedly. "We can ride along there and cut him off at the bridge!"

"Good!" said Otto, "But you must promise not to try to capture him. Just delay him. Meantime I'll call the police."

The children agreed and piled into the pony cart. Henry took the reins, slapped them hard, and steered Daisy down a wide path through the woods.

The cart bounced, and the riders held on tightly. But they reached the foot of the hill safely.

"Giddap there, Daisy!" Henry cried, and the animal trotted off briskly along the stream.

"Do you think we'll make it, Henry?" Nan asked anxiously.

"We have a good chance. This road goes straight to the bridge, but the lane Skinny's taking winds all around first."

"I wonder why he stole those signs," said Flossie.

"Just to be mean, I guess," said Henry. "He's always snitching something."

Freddie looked anxious. "What are we going to do to stop him?"

"Make a roadblock," said Bert. "We'll park the cart crossways and all get out."

"There are lots of bushes near the bridge where we can hide," said Henry.

"That's a good plan!" Nan agreed. "I just

hope the police get there before Skinny moves your cart."

"Can you go any faster?" Nellie asked worriedly. "We don't want to miss him."

"Giddap!" Henry cried.

More dust flew up from Daisy's hoofs, and the children hung on tighter as the cart sped onward. Suddenly they rounded a bend and some distance ahead saw an open bridge over the small river. Leading straight onto the span was a lane which crossed the road they were on.

"Look!" cried Flossie.

A shiny black buggy, pulled by a fast-trotting horse, was coming across the bridge. A tall boy held the reins. Beside him sat a little girl about five years old, wearing a long pink dress and a white cap.

The next moment the children heard the roar of a car coming toward them. "It's Skinny!" Freddie cried excitedly. "Hurry! Hurry!"

"Giddap!" shouted Henry and Daisy sprinted toward the crossroad. Just as the Amish buggy rolled off the bridge, Skinny's car came rattling up to it.

"He's going to hit the buggy!" Nellie exclaimed.

The children shouted for Skinny to stop, but the beat-up car turned toward the bridge. The frightened horse bolted down the embankment into the stream, dragging the buggy with it. The vehicle overturned with a loud splash. The little girl screamed.

Moments later the pony cart reached the lane. By this time Skinny was already across the bridge. Picking up speed, he passed them and disappeared down the road.

The Bobbsey group jumped out and splashed into the shallow water where the Amish boy was helping the little girl to her feet.

"Are you hurt?" Nan cried.

The boy shook his head. He had long dark hair and black eyes. "Just wet," he said quietly. He turned to the little girl, who was crying. "What is it, Rachel?"

"My knee hurts," she sobbed.

Nan put an arm around her. "Come, dear," she said, leading her to the shore. "Sit down here on the grass and let us look at it."

Rachel raised her long dress and the other girls saw that her bare knee was skinned. Nan took a clean handkerchief from her pocket, dipped it in the stream and gently washed the wound.

"It's just a scrape," she said, patting the little girl's hand. "It'll be all right."

Meanwhile the boys had helped the floundering horse to its feet and put the buggy upright.

"This is keen," said Bert, patting the shiny black side of the vehicle.

"It's my courting buggy," said the stranger as

he stooped to pick his black hat out of the stream. He explained that when an Amish boy reaches the age of sixteen his parents buy him a buggy in which to take out girls.

Freddie made a face. "You mean that's all you do with this cool buggy? You just ride around with girls?"

The boys smiled. "That's what it's for. When I get married and have a family I will have a larger carriage. Today I was giving my little sister a ride."

Bert introduced himself, Freddie, and Henry. The Amish boy told them his name was Amos Shrucker.

"I saw you at the barn-raising," he said shyly. Then he turned anxiously and looked over the carriage.

Henry said, "I don't think it's hurt much. There are some bad scratches here on the side, but I guess you can fix those."

With the others helping, Amos guided the horse and buggy out of the stream.

"I wish we could ride in that," Flossie whispered to Nan.

Amos heard her and smiled. "Why not? Your brother could drive you across the bridge and back."

Grinning, Bert climbed up and took the reins. Nan seated herself next to him, and Amos swung Flossie up between them. Then he lifted Fred-

"Hold tight on the harness," Amos told Freddie

die onto the horse's back. "Hold tight to the harness," he told him.

"You can take a turn next," he said to Nellie and Henry as the buggy took off briskly across the bridge. In a few minutes it came back with the Bobbseys waving and laughing.

"Oh, that was such fun!" Flossie said. "Thank you a lot."

The others echoed her thanks. After Henry and Nellie had taken their turn, the Amish boy lifted Rachel into the buggy.

"We'll go home now," he said, then turned to the children. "Thank you for helping us."

"That's all right," said Nan. "I'm glad you weren't hurt."

"Why don't you come see us some time?" Henry asked. "Everybody knows where Cloverbank is."

Rachel smiled shyly and looked at her brother, then folded her hands in her lap.

"We don't go out much," said Amos quietly. "But we will see." He slapped the reins and drove off.

Nan sighed. "We lost the hex sign and Skinny after all."

A black police car drove up. Bert hurried over and told the two officers what had happened.

"We'll see if we can pick up Skinny," the driver said, and started off.

The children climbed into the pony cart and headed for Otto's house. After reporting to him, they drove back to Cloverbank.

Aunt Doris was in the barn lining a large black trunk with flowered wallpaper. Nearby were a small red leather trunk and two big ones with bright shiny locks. When Mrs. Zoop saw the gift Nan and Nellie had brought, she hugged them.

"It's just wonderful!" she said. "And to think that it once belonged at Cloverbank!"

Her smile faded when the children told her about their adventure with Skinny Broome. Aunt Doris shook her head. "I certainly hope the police find that man."

But when Uncle Walter called the police at suppertime, the peddler was still at large. During the evening the children told stories on the back porch. It was hot and no breeze stirred. Heavy clouds gathered.

"It gives *donnerwetter,*" said Freddie.

But the storm did not break until much later. When Freddie got into the lower bunk bed a flash of lightning streaked across the sky, casting a weird glow in the dark room. Thunder rumbled.

"I hope that old prowler doesn't come around tonight," the little boy said.

"Don't worry," his brother answered. "Uncle Walter locked all the doors."

As Bert climbed into the top bunk, he noticed that Henry was still seated on his cot.

"What's the matter?" he asked.

"Uh, nothing," Henry replied vaguely. "I just happened to think of something." He put on his slippers and robe. "I'm kind of hungry. Would anybody else like an apple?"

Freddie sat up again quickly. "I would!"

"Yes, me too," put in Bert.

"Okay," said Henry. "I'll go get some." He started for the door.

Bert called, "Wait! I'll go with you."

"No!" said Henry quickly. "Don't bother. I'll be right up again." As he hurried out, the door hinges squeaked.

Bert sat up in bed and stared into the darkness, thinking about the mystery. "I wish we hadn't lost that Cloverbank hex sign," he said.

"I wonder what Skinny Broome thought he would do with it," Freddie spoke up. "It's not much good any more. It's all dirty and burned."

"I think he wanted the new sign that was on the table," Bert said. "He probably picked up the old one just because it was next to it."

A few minutes later Henry returned with three apples.

"Leave the door partway open," said Bert, "so we get some breeze."

The boys sat in the dark listening to the storm

while they ate the apples. Then they put the cores in the wastebasket and lay down. Before long the two older ones were asleep.

But Freddie stayed awake. Suddenly he thought, "What was that noise?" His heart skipped a beat. Someone was coming down the hall! Suppose the prowler had entered the house!

The bedroom door squeaked open!

Too frightened to speak, Freddie closed his eyes. The next moment he heard a soft step on the carpet. Then something cold and wet and soft brushed his face!

CHAPTER XI

SUSPICIOUS NOISES

FREDDIE gave a frightened cry. He opened his eyes and saw a white woolly head close to his own. Sheela, the sheep!

"What's the matter?" Bert asked, sitting up.

At the same moment Henry awoke and saw the animal beside the bed.

The sheep nuzzled Freddie again, and he giggled. "Hey, cut it out! You're tickling me!"

Bert reached over and turned on a lamp near him. The sheep looked up, blinking.

"How did she get up here?" Bert asked.

Henry hopped out of bed and went over to his pet. "She got scared of the thunder, I guess."

He confessed that when he went downstairs he had propped open the screen door so that Sheela could come into the house if she were frightened of the storm. "Usually she stays in the kitchen," said Henry. "I don't know why she came upstairs this time."

"There was some pretty loud thunder," Freddie remarked. "Maybe she got scared."

"We'd better get her downstairs fast," said Henry. "I don't want my mother to find her."

"I'll help you," Bert volunteered.

"Me, too," said Freddie.

"No," his brother told him. "Three of us will make too much noise. You stay here."

The two boys put on raincoats, hats, and boots. Then Henry took the sheep by the collar and led her toward the door. She went willingly out of the room and down the hall. But she balked at the top of the stairs.

"She's not used to these steps," Henry whispered. "I'll go first and sort of hold her up."

Bert nodded and clutched the rear end of the sheep, trying to steady her as Henry began to pull Sheela downstairs. Haltingly, the two boys and the sheep took several steps. But halfway down, Sheela let out a low *baaa.*

"Shh! Quiet!" Bert whispered.

"Come on, Sheela girl," Henry coaxed. He pulled and Bert pushed, but Sheela tried to stand fast. Suddenly her back legs slipped and her front legs flew out from under her!

THUMP! THUMP! THUMP! The two boys and the sheep skidded down the stairs and landed in a heap at the bottom!

"Baaa!" cried Sheela loudly and scrambled to her feet.

THUMP! THUMP! THUMP!

Henry sat up dazedly. "You okay, Bert?" he asked.

"Yes, I'm all right. But that did it! Everybody in the house will be down here in one second."

Bert sat up, straightened his rain hat, and quickly got to his feet. To the boys' surprise, no one appeared.

"I guess everybody's too sound asleep," said Henry. "We're lucky."

Again they grasped Sheela and started moving her along the hall toward the kitchen.

Suddenly Henry stopped short. "Wait!" he said softly. "I thought I heard a footstep in the kitchen."

"Maybe someone else is up," Bert suggested.

"I hope it isn't my mother or father," said Henry worriedly. "I'm not supposed to leave the door open at night for Sheela, but she gets so scared when it storms, I feel sorry for her."

Both boys listened, but could hear no sound except the rain beating against the windows.

"Are you sure you heard somebody?" Bert asked.

"Maybe not," said Henry. "Come on! We'd better put Sheela in her shelter."

The two boys led the sheep across the kitchen, her hoofs clacking on the linoleum. They guided her through the open screen door, down the porch steps, and into her pen. Henry took Sheela into the wooden shed at the rear of it and tethered her to a stake in the ground.

"There's nothing to be afraid of now, old girl," Henry said softly. "You'll be okay."

Meanwhile, Bert was looking around the yard. Through the darkness and rain he could see the dim shape of the barn, and the smokehouse beside it.

Suddenly there came a flash of lightning. Bert thought he saw a figure slip into the smokehouse! Henry came out of the shed and Bert told him what he had seen.

"Are you sure?" Henry asked, alarmed. "I'll go tell Dad right away."

"No! Wait a minute!" said Bert. "We'd better be certain before you wake your father."

The boys slipped out of the pen and hurried toward the dark smokehouse. As they stopped a few feet from the partly opened door, they heard soft talking inside.

Suddenly a deep, harsh voice burst out, "You fool! That hex sign might be a clue! And you sold it!" Fox's voice!

"How was I to know that?" replied a whining voice. "I thought it was a piece of junk. Besides, how do you know it could be a clue?"

"I told you, Skinny," Fox replied angrily. "I heard those kids talking in their room."

"Seems to me they know more than you do," Skinny muttered. "And what's worse, we can't get away from them. They're all over the place!"

"I know," said Fox bitterly. "I was minding my own business looking over an Amish buggy at the auction, and who climbs into it? That little blond boy!"

"And his sister came peeking through the lattice under the porch when you were searching for an exit to the passage," said Skinny. He sighed. "Sometimes I think there isn't any secret tunnel."

"There has to be," said Fox grimly, "and I know I could find it if those kids would let us alone."

At that moment a flash of lightning bathed the boys in white light. A hoarse cry came from the smokehouse.

"There they are again!" Fox exclaimed. "Come on! Beat it!"

The boys heard a scrambling noise.

"They're climbing out the back through the ruined wall!" Henry cried out.

As the boys darted around the smokehouse, another flash of lightning lit up the yard. They could see the two men in raincoats and hats running toward the springhouse. A moment later they disappeared inside.

"Now we've got them!" Bert gloated. "I'll bolt the door so they can't get out and you go for help."

"They're not trapped," said Henry. Quickly he explained that the stone house was built in two halves with a covered corridor between. "That's where the men went. The spring is there in a rocky pit. They can run right past it and out into the Lower Meadow."

"Then come on," said Bert. "Let's try to stop them!"

The boys raced to the springhouse and into the corridor. Bert stopped on the narrow walk beside the pit.

"Henry, you'd better go back and tell your father."

"Okay. But first we ought to look in the storage room. They might have gone in there."

Quietly he opened a door near the entrance and they peered in. It was too dark to see anything. All was silent. Suddenly another flash of lightning lit the bare room. No one was in sight. Bert closed the door again.

"Straight across the meadow is a side road," Henry explained. "They're probably heading for that."

"Maybe I can hold 'em up somehow," said Bert, and ran on through the corridor out into the rain.

He dashed down a steep flight of stone steps to a wooden gate. Opening it, Bert strained his eyes toward the edge of the field where heavy brush grew along the fence.

"The road must be beyond there," he thought.

Bert peered through the darkness but could spot no one anywhere. He listened and heard only the splashing rain. Where had the men gone? And what was taking Henry so long?

Suddenly Bert caught a sound. Brush was crackling close by the road. He moved toward it.

Crack! Someone was sneaking through the bushes.

As Bert crept forward, he made out two dark figures climbing the fence. Moments later car headlights flashed on and it roared away.

"The men got away!" Bert thought.

Disappointed, he turned and sloshed back across the meadow to the springhouse. Making his way through the corridor, he wondered again where Henry and Uncle Walter were.

Bert went out into the yard and stopped short. What was that pounding noise? It seemed to be coming from the ruined bakehouse.

Warily he walked to the stone building. The door hung on one hinge. Cautiously Bert pushed it open.

As his eyes became accustomed to the gloom, he saw a large brick oven built into the wall. The noise was coming from there!

CHAPTER XII

THE TIN CLUE

BERT'S heart thumped with excitement. Who was pounding? Should he open the oven door and see?

"If I could peek in first," he thought, "it would be safer." Looking for a hole in the brick work, he stepped around to the side. Most of the oven wall was broken away. Caught inside was a struggling figure!

"Henry!" Bert exclaimed. The boy was gagged and his hands and feet tied together. Quickly Bert freed him and helped Henry climb out.

"Boy, what happened to you?" he asked.

"When you left me, Dr. Fox clapped a hand over my mouth and yanked me into the storage room. Skinny tied me up and carried me in here."

"Where was he hiding?" Bert asked.

"I forgot about the trench at the far end of the storage room," Henry confessed. "It's a long pit, and water from the spring runs into it. In the old days people put jugs of milk in it to keep them cool."

"They probably heard us talking," said Bert, "and figured they'd throw a scare into us."

"That's right," Henry agreed. "One of them said, 'Maybe this will teach you not to be so nosy!' " Henry doubled up his fists. "Just wait. I'll show them!" He swung his arm. "Pow!"

Bert grinned. "But first we have to catch them! Let's go and tell your father."

The boys ran across the yard in the rain. Just then a light went on in the kitchen. When they walked in, everyone was there in slippers and robes.

"Where were you?" Aunt Doris asked.

Freddie spoke up. "When you didn't come back, I got worried, so I told Uncle Walter."

Nan said, "We heard Freddic, too, so we all came down to look for you."

Quickly the boys told what had happened. Mr. Zoop hurried off to phone the police asking them to be on the lookout for the men's car.

"I'm not surprised to hear that Skinny Broome is mixed up in this," Nan remarked as her twin and Henry took off their muddy boots. "It's just like him."

"Fox was probably searching the mystery room when Sheela came upstairs," said Bert. "I guess he got scared by us and the sheep and sneaked downstairs ahead of us."

Henry grinned and told the others that the prowlers had been arguing when they tied him up. "Fox said Skinny was too chicken to come into the house with him."

When Mr. Zoop returned, he spoke sternly to his son. "After this you're not to leave doors open at night. Sheela must stay in her shelter."

"I know," said Henry. "I'm sorry."

"Now everybody back to bed!" said Uncle Walter.

By morning the rain had stopped and the sky was bright blue. After a delicious Sunday dinner, Bert suggested that the detectives retrace the prowlers' steps. "Maybe we'll be lucky and find a clue."

Freddie and Flossie said they would rather play with Jiffy Jay, but the other three followed Bert upstairs.

"There was a trail of muddy splotches all the way from the kitchen door to the mystery room," said Nellie, "but Aunt Doris cleaned them up this morning."

The children searched carefully, but found no other clue to the intruder.

"From here he went out to the smokehouse," said Henry. "Let's try there. Get some flashlights."

The children hurried to the yard. Watching

the ground for evidence, they crossed to the stone building and stepped inside. It was gloomy except for the little sunlight which came through the broken place in the back wall.

"It smells of smoke," said Nellie.

"Course it does," said Henry. "This is where people used to hang hams and bacon in the old days. Then they built a hickory wood fire underneath and the smoke cured the meat." He pointed upward and the children saw wooden rafters with hooks where the smoked meat had been hung.

"But that was years ago," said Nellie.

"It doesn't matter," her cousin replied. "The smell of smoke lasts a long time."

The children searched the earthen floor but found nothing. Next they went to the storage room in the springhouse.

"This is where they gagged and tied me," Henry announced.

"Where did they get the gag and the rope?" Nan wanted to know.

"Fox had a handkerchief in his pocket," said Henry, "and they found the ropes in the corner."

"Let's look this place over carefully for clues," said Bert.

Each of the four young detectives took a section of the room. Nellie chose the big open fireplace. Beside it stood a long, low box with painted flowers on it.

"What was this for?" Nellie asked.

"Wood," said Henry. "In the old days, people kept logs and kindling on hand for the fireplaces."

Twenty minutes later every inch of the stone floor had been examined, including the milk trench.

"Not a single clue!" said Nellie with a sigh.

"There's one place we haven't looked," said Nan. "Under the wood box. This floor is not even and something could have rolled beneath the box."

"It won't hurt to look," said Bert. The four moved the heavy box away from the wall.

"Hey! There's a clue!" cried Nan.

"It's a key chain," said Bert, picking it up, "but there are no keys on it."

"There's a metal disk, though. What does that say?" Henry asked.

Bert examined the tin medallion which hung on the chain. "It says *Tonkin the Tinsmith, Paradise, Pennsylvania.*"

Nellie looked puzzled. "What's Mr. Tonkin's key chain doing here?"

"It might not be his," Bert said. "This looks to me like an advertising gimmick."

"This is just about where they gagged and tied me," Henry put in. "Maybe Dr. Fox pulled

"Hey! There's a clue!" Nan cried

it out of his pocket with the handkerchief. I struggled pretty hard, and I guess this was kicked under the wood box."

"You're probably right," said Nellie, "because it's new and shiny. It couldn't have been here long."

"This is worth following," said Bert. "Tonkin might be the man who bought the hex sign from Skinny."

"And even if he isn't, he might be able to give us a clue to where Skinny and Dr. Fox can be found," Nan said.

The children hurried back to the house. After asking permission of Aunt Doris, Bert telephoned the tinsmith in Paradise. The others listened eagerly while he talked.

When he hung up Bert said, "Mr. Tonkin is not at home, but his brother says he'll be back late this afternoon."

"In that case, I'll drive you down there," Aunt Doris volunteered. "Paradise is not far from here."

Freddie and Flossie came down the hall from the kitchen and joined them.

"Oh, may we go, too?" Flossie asked eagerly.

"Everyone can go," said Aunt Doris with a smile. "You'll like the train ride."

"Train!" the visitors chorused.

"I thought we were going in the car," said Freddie.

Henry grinned. "Only as far as Strasburg. From there to Paradise we'll take the steam locomotive."

Flossie clapped her hands. "You mean a real old-time choo-choo?"

"That's right," said Aunt Doris.

In a short time the station wagon was winding along narrow roads past large well-kept farms.

Bert looked worried. "Skinny and Fox might be on their way to see Tonkin right this minute in order to get the hex sign back."

"Maybe Tonkin is not the man who bought it from Skinny," Nan reminded him.

"I hope he is, though," said Bert. "If somebody else bought it, we haven't a chance to get the sign before Skinny does. He and Fox will have the clue to the secret passage and we won't."

"Cheer up. Remember, it might not be a clue, after all," said Nellie.

Half an hour later Aunt Doris pulled into a parking lot back of a small, old-fashioned railroad station. It was a yellow frame building trimmed in red. The children ran around to the front, where the tracks were. An old-time locomotive with three coaches stood there. Suddenly the whistle blew.

"Hurry now and catch it," said Aunt Doris. "I'll drive to Paradise and meet you at the end of the line."

While Bert raced back to buy tickets, the other children piled onto the train.

"Oh, it's great!" exclaimed Freddie. "Just like in old-time Western movies!"

"Maybe Indians will shoot arrows through the windows," said Nan, giggling.

"This used to be Indian country," Henry said.

The twins and their friends sat on blue plush seats across the aisle from a little old-fashioned stove. Next to it stood a tall coal bucket.

"It's a real stove," Henry told them, "and in the wintertime it burns coal."

Bert came dashing into the car and gave out the long paper tickets. Then a handsome young man in a conductor's uniform came through the coach. The children turned to watch as he stood on the platform between the cars and picked up a microphone.

"Ladies and gentlemen, you are now on the Cannonball Express. It leaves at four o'clock promptly, or as soon as it can get going!"

Everyone laughed. A few minutes later, there was another blast on the whistle. The train lurched and with a *chug-chug-chug* started down the track.

Joking as he talked, the conductor told the passengers that they were going forty miles an hour and it would take fifteen minutes to reach Paradise.

After a while the young twins walked to the

door and looked into the last car, which was open-sided with only railings. Down the middle stood two long benches, back to back. A stout man in a green shirt was seated on one of them. He was the only passenger.

"Let's ride out there," said Freddie.

He and Flossie made their way across the lurching platform past the conductor. For a few minutes they stood at the railing, looking across the cornfields.

"Oh!" Flossie exclaimed, and pointed to a road beyond them. "That looks like Skinny's car!"

Just then the automobile disappeared behind a row of trees. Flossie climbed onto the bench, hoping to spot it again.

"Can you see it? Is the car really Skinny's?" Freddie asked excitedly.

"It is! It is!" Flossie told him. "There are two people in it."

"We should tell the others!" Freddie cried. He raced toward the end of the car.

Flossie, forgetting about the stout man, ran along the bench.

"Ouch!" he yelled as Flossie stumbled across his lap.

With a cry, the little girl went flying off the bench!

CHAPTER XIII

A FLOATING STONE

"HEY there! Watch it!" exclaimed the conductor, leaping forward. He caught Flossie and kept her from falling off the train. "Take it easy!"

"Yes!" said the fat man crossly. "Why don't you walk on the floor instead of the bench?"

Tears came to Flossie's eyes. "I'm s-sorry." Then she turned to the conductor. "Thank you for catching me."

"Glad to do it!" said the young man. "Don't cry, but from now on keep your feet on the floor."

Flossie promised. Then she hurried after her twin into the next car. Quickly they told about the automobile. The other children pressed their noses to the windows and looked across the fields toward the road.

"I think you're right," said Bert. "That does look like Skinny's old junk. I'll bet he and Fox are on the way to the same place we are."

Anxiously the children watched as the car pulled ahead of the slow-moving train. By the time the Cannon Ball Express reached the railroad yard at Paradise, the automobile was nowhere to be seen.

As the worried children got off the train, they saw the Zoop station wagon parked near the siding. They ran over and quickly told Aunt Doris their news.

"Better hurry then," she said and pointed across the street to a white house with a sign in the yard. It said *Tonkin, Tinsmith.*

The young detectives ran over and went up the steps onto the big front porch. Nan rang the bell. The door was opened by a thin man with a mop of curly brown hair. His bright brown eyes opened wide with surprise when he saw the six children.

"What can I do for you?" he asked.

Swiftly Bert told him who they were and what they wanted.

"Oh, yes. My brother told me you called on the telephone," he said. "Funny you should come about that sign. The fellow I bought it from was chust here fifteen minutes ago. He wanted to buy it back."

"Did you sell it back to him?" chorused the children.

"No. I didn't have it any more." Mr. Tonkin

shook his head. "*Ach!* You should have seen the peddler when I told him the hex was gone. Such a sour face he made!"

"Where is the sign?" Nan asked quickly.

"I sold it yesterday to a couple of tourists," the tinsmith replied.

"Who are they?" Bert asked. "How can we find them?"

The tinsmith chuckled. "Hold your horses! What's so special about this sign?"

Nan briefly told him of the two stolen hexes. Mr. Tonkin gave a low whistle. "*Ach,* too bad!"

He said that the peddler had stopped him on the street in Lancaster and sold him both signs. Later Mr. Tonkin had gone to the market. "The tourists saw me there with the big new hex under my arm. They wanted to buy it, so I sold it to them and threw in the old sign.

"Their name is Barton—a young man and his wife. I don't know where you can find them, but they did say they were going to visit Cornwall Furnace tomorrow."

"What do they look like?" Freddie asked.

Mr. Tonkin said both were blond, and the husband had worn a blue sports jacket.

"That should be some help," Bert remarked, then looked worried. "Did you tell all this to the peddler?"

Mr. Tonkin nodded. "Yes. I'm sorry if I did wrong."

"That's all right," said Flossie kindly. "You didn't know he was a bad man."

The children thanked the tinsmith, hurried back to the car and reported to Mrs. Zoop.

"Well, we still have a chance," she said. "I'll drive you to Cornwall Furnace first thing tomorrow morning."

"Oh, Aunt Doris, you're wonderful!" exclaimed Nan as the others thanked her too.

"You're such good detectives," said Henry's mother, "it would be a shame not to help you."

Early Monday morning Aunt Doris drove the children to the nearby town of Lebanon. On the outskirts they followed a narrow road beside a stream, then up a hill. At the top lay two long buildings made of red sandstone. They had narrow, high, pointed windows.

"That's where we're going," said Henry.

"Where's the furnace?" Freddie asked.

"Inside," Henry replied. "It's not a furnace like in your house. This one is very big and was used to get the iron out of iron ore. In the old days this place made cannon balls for George Washington's navy."

Nellie looked surprised. "I didn't know he had a navy."

"Sure he did," said Henry. "The Colonies had seven ships they used during the Revolution."

A few minutes later, Aunt Doris parked in the

lot beside the building. There were several other cars, but none was Skinny's old one.

"I'll wait for you here," said Mrs. Zoop.

Henry led the way through a heavy wooden door into the nearest building, which was gloomy. The floor and walls were made of stone.

"This is kind of like a castle," Freddie whispered.

A round-faced man in a gray sweater stepped from an inner room and offered to show them around.

"Thank you. We're looking for some people," Nan added. She described the young tourists, and Fox and Skinny.

"They may be here," the man replied. "Some folks go around without a guide. We'll see."

As the children followed him, he explained that they were in the storage house. Iron ore had been mined nearby and put here. Along the walls were lighted glass cases showing samples of the cannon balls and other objects which had been made there long ago. In one corner were large pieces of rough-looking rock.

"What big stones!" said Nellie. "I'll bet they're awfully heavy."

The guide's pink face creased into a smile. "Try to pick one up," he said.

Nellie looked doubtful, but lifted the top piece. "Why, it hardly weighs anything!"

"Bring it here," said the guide, going over to a tub of water. "Toss it in!"

Nellie dropped the big lump of gray stuff into the water.

"It floats!" cried Flossie as the other children exclaimed in surprise.

"A floating stone!" said Nellie.

Bert grinned. "What is it?"

"It's not really stone, of course," the guide said. "It's slag."

"What's that?" Freddie asked.

"Well, iron ore is put down in the furnace," the man explained. "When the ore gets hot, the iron melts and runs out. What is left afterwards is this lightweight chunk called slag."

The children watched, fascinated, as the big gray lump slowly sank.

"It has lots of holes in it, like a honeycomb," the man went on. "As soon as one fills with water, it sinks."

He led them along a covered walk to the next building. "Here's the furnace," he said and pointed to a large hole in the floor covered by a piece of glass. "The ore was brought here in carts, weighed and dropped down this hole with a load of lime and one of charcoal."

"Why is there glass over it now?" asked Freddie.

"So little boys can't fall into it," the man replied with a smile. "The furnace goes down sev-

"A floating stone!" said Nellie

eral stories to the bottom floor where the iron ran out. But it doesn't work any more. This place is just a museum now."

As he was talking, Nan drifted to a side door and stepped out onto a wooden stairway. Below was a huge pit lit by a red light. In it she saw a water wheel several stories high. Skinny and Fox were on a balcony overlooking the pit!

"They're here!" Nan cried to the others. "Come quick!"

The children dashed over and looked down. Henry was so excited he could not keep still. "There they are!" he shouted. "Call the police!"

The men looked up startled, and the next moment darted through an archway behind the balcony.

"Now you've done it!" cried Bert. "After them, everybody!"

"What's going on?" cried the guide, but the children were already racing down the steps into the pit.

They dashed up the stairs onto the balcony and through the arch after the two men! But the slippery pair escaped to the parking lot and drove off in a black sedan.

Aunt Doris had the motor running when the children reached the station wagon. "I couldn't stop them," she said. "They dashed right past me and jumped into their car. A blond man and woman left just before them in a blue convertible."

"The tourists!" Nan exclaimed. "Oh, let's go after them, Aunt Doris!"

As the station wagon roared out of the parking lot, Mrs. Zoop remarked that the men did not have the sign with them. "They probably haven't made contact with the tourists yet."

Reaching the highway, the Bobbsey party could see the black sedan ahead following the blue convertible. The station wagon tailed them to the small town of Ephrata.

"The Bartons must be heading for the old cloister," said Henry. He explained that this was a village where certain religious pioneers had lived.

"Some of the original buildings are still standing," said Aunt Doris. "Others have been restored."

In a few minutes she turned into the parking lot beside a group of gray frame houses with peaked roofs.

"The tourists are here!" Bert cried excitedly. He pointed across the lot to the blue car.

"So are the bad men!" said Freddie. "There's Skinny's jalopy!"

"Oh, I hope they haven't found the Bartons already!" Nellie said anxiously.

Everyone piled out, including Aunt Doris.

They hurried into the main building and bought tickets.

"I think we'd better separate," said Bert as they stepped outside. "As soon as you see the Bartons, give a double whistle." The others agreed and hastened off to search.

Freddie headed along a walk toward a tall frame house. Against one side wall was a stairway leading to a small flagstone yard.

Halfway down the steps Freddie stopped in surprise. On a stone platform adjoining the stairs was a fat jar, almost as tall as he was.

Curious, the little boy stepped over and stared into the wide mouth of the jar. It was empty.

Just then a deep voice said, "I saw those twins again. We'd better find the tourists before they do!"

Dr. Fox.

Freddie glanced up the stairs and saw a pair of big feet in brown shoes coming down. Behind them was a smaller pair in old loafers!

Quick as a wink, Freddie scrambled into the big jar and crouched down. The footsteps passed and went away. He stood up and tried to climb out of the jar. It began to tip! Quickly he dropped down again and the jar settled back.

Freddie was frightened. "How will I ever get out of this?" he wondered.

CHAPTER XIV

AN OLD TUNNEL

"HELP!" Freddie yelled.

Then he gave the whistle signal. Once more he tried to climb out of the big jar, but as he pulled himself up on the wide rim, it rocked. He could imagine the jar falling off its stone platform, crashing down the stairs and breaking into a million pieces.

"And me too," he thought.

In a minute he heard the other children talking. "Where are you, Freddie?" came Nan's voice.

"In the jar!" he called. Footsteps sounded on the stone stairs.

"What are you doing in there?" Bert asked as he and the others ran down.

"I was hiding from the bad men," said Freddie. "The tourists left and they went after them."

"Oh dear," said Nan, sighing.

Bert and Henry tipped the jar carefully onto its side and Freddie crawled out. After the boys had set the jar upright again, the six children raced up the steps and along the path to the parking lot. Both the tourists' car and the black sedan were gone!

Aunt Doris waved from the station wagon, and the children dashed over to her. "I just got here," she said quickly. "I spotted Dr. Fox and Skinny leaving."

"We know," said Bert. "The tourists are gone, too. But where?"

Mrs. Zoop thought a moment. "Landis Valley Farm Museum is a big attraction for visitors. Maybe they went there."

"Is that far from here?" Nellie asked.

"No," her aunt replied, "and it's worth a try. Jump in!" The children piled into the station wagon and they started off.

At the edge of town, Mrs. Zoop pulled into a service station. "Sorry, but we'll have to stop for gas."

Henry groaned. "If Skinny and Fox catch up to the tourists before we do, they'll get the hex sign and then they'll have the clue to the secret passage and the treasure and everything!"

"If it *is* a clue," said Nellie. "Remember, we're not sure."

"No, but there's a good chance the hex sign

can help us find the passage," said Bert. "We've just got to get it back!"

"I'm kind of hungry," said Freddie, spotting a delicatessen next door. "Why don't we buy sandwiches and take them along?"

"Good idea," said Aunt Doris. "Get fruit and cookies, too." She gave Nan some money.

Ten minutes later they were on the road again, munching sandwiches and watching for a glimpse of the black sedan or the tourists' car. They had just finished their cookies when Aunt Doris turned down a driveway. She stopped in front of a large brick building.

A tall man in farm clothes stepped out and leaned into the open window of the station wagon. "Welcome to Landis Valley, folks. You can park over on the side if you want to go into the museum."

"We're really looking for someone," Aunt Doris replied.

Bert described the tourists, then added, "I don't see their car anywhere. Have they been here?"

The farmer nodded. "They looked around for a little while and then went on. The man asked me about a good place to stay in Lebanon, so I guess that's where they're heading." He named a hotel.

"Those folks must be very popular," he added. "Two men were asking for them also.

Maybe you know them. They're driving a black car."

"We know them all right!" put in Henry. "And we wish we didn't!"

The Bobbsey party thanked the man for his help and went on. A little later they drove into Lebanon. Suddenly they heard a loud *clank!*

"What's that?" asked Aunt Doris, frowning.

"It's in the motor," Henry spoke up, as the noise came again.

"I'd better take the car to a garage and see what's the matter," Mrs. Zoop said.

In a few minutes Nan pointed to a large hotel on the corner. "There's the place the man at Landis Valley told us about."

"I'm afraid to stop," Aunt Doris replied, "because I might not get the car started again. I'll keep going until we find a garage, and you can walk back. By the way," she added, "that's the hotel that was robbed a couple of weeks ago."

A little farther on she pulled into a service station and the children hurried back to the hotel. Bert explained to the desk clerk that they were looking for the Bartons and described the young couple.

"They're not registered here," he said.

"Maybe they went sightseeing first," Nan suggested.

"Go to the tourist bureau in the basement,"

the clerk suggested. "They'll give you a full list of the attractions around here."

Downstairs in a corridor of shops the children found the tourist office. A pretty girl with short brown hair waited on them. Bert described the Bartons and asked if they had been there.

The girl nodded. "Yes. About half an hour ago."

"Do you know where they went?" Nellie asked eagerly.

"Probably to the Union Canal Tunnel," the girl replied. "They were interested in that, because it's the oldest tunnel in the United States. It was built in 1827. Canals used to carry lots of passengers and freight," she went on, "but when the steam locomotive was invented, railroads put them out of business."

"I guess the trains replaced the covered wagons, too," Bert remarked.

While the girl told the older children how to find the tunnel, Flossie and Freddie slipped out, and strolled down the hall. They stopped to look in the open door of a barber shop. It was empty except for the plump barber, who was reading a magazine.

He glanced up and smiled. "Want a haircut?"

"No, thanks," said Freddie. He spotted a mechanical horse just inside the door. "I'd like a ride on that."

"Go ahead," said the barber.

Freddie dug into his pocket and took out a coin. Quickly he climbed into the saddle and stuck the money into a slot in a box beside the animal. With a whirr of the motor the horse began to rock back and forth.

"Yippee!" cried Freddie. "Ride 'em cowboy!" As he flung one hand into the air the bronco suddenly bucked harder.

"Yow!" yelled Freddie, slipping sideways in the saddle.

"Catch him!" cried Flossie. She and the barber leaped for Freddie and steadied him.

"Take it easy, Tex!" said the barber. "You kids alone?"

"No," said Flossie and explained about the others.

"We're d-d-detectives," said Freddie while the bronco bucked.

The man grinned. "I hope you're not investigating the hotel robbery. I told all I know."

Freddie looked surprised. "D-did you see it happen?"

"Sure did," replied the barber. "I was in the lobby and saw the thieves make their getaway. One was tall and blond and the other was a little thin guy. Both had masks on."

"They sound just like the bad men we're looking for," said Flossie.

"Yeah?" said the barber, chuckling. "Well,

"Yow!" yelled Freddie

you can forget those two. They're far from here by now—unless they've got rocks in their heads. Funny thing, though," he added. "A little while ago a tall, dark-haired guy passed my door. He was built just like the big blond thief."

"I'll bet it was Dr. Fox," said Freddie excitedly, when the horse stopped bucking. "He has a dark wig."

The barber smiled. "Kid, you've got a great imagination!"

Just then the other children came down the hall. As Freddie slipped from the saddle, Bert called to the young twins, "Come on! Hurry! We have to get out to the Union Canal Tunnel."

Freddie and Flossie said good-by to the barber and hurried from the shop.

"I just hope we're not too late," said Nellie anxiously.

As they ran upstairs, she told the younger twins that Fox and Skinny had also been to the tourist bureau and had learned where the Bartons were going.

Excitedly Freddie and Flossie repeated what the barber had told them. "Skinny and Fox are the hotel thieves," he said, "but the barber said they'd be far away by now."

"The barber's right," said Bert, as they trotted along the sidewalk. "Those robbers are probably miles away by now."

A few minutes later they reported to Aunt Doris at the garage.

"The car is in bad shape," she said, "and it won't be fixed until tomorrow. I'll call Daddy and arrange for us to stay at the hotel tonight."

"That'll be fun," said Flossie, clapping her hands. Then she added quickly, "But how will we get to the tunnel?"

"You can rent bikes here," Mrs. Zoop said. "I'll meet you at the hotel for supper. If you see Fox and Skinny," she warned, "don't try to tackle them alone. Go for the police."

The children promised, and ten minutes later were pedaling up a side road, with Bert in the lead. Soon they reached the small gravel parking lot at the top of a hill.

"This is the place," said Bert.

"No cars here," remarked Henry. "Maybe we're too late."

The children looked out over the wide valley of farmland below. Bert said, "I see a road down there. Maybe the tourists are coming that way. We'd better go and check."

They left their bicycles and filed down a stone stairway into a steep, narrow path. High shrubs grew on both sides.

"It's spooky," said Flossie. Her voice rang out clearly. "I wish we had policemen with us, 'cause maybe the bad men are down there."

"Shh!" said Bert softly. "If they are, we don't want them to know we're coming."

After a few minutes the Bobbseys and their

friends reached level ground. Before them lay a wide lagoon.

"I guess this is what's left of the old canal," said Nan quietly.

"And there's the tunnel!" Freddie whispered.

Behind them, under the hill they had just come down, was the entrance to a large brick tunnel. Although the shadows were deep inside it, the water near the opening was green and slimy. At the far end were the sun-dappled leaves of thick brush.

The children turned to look around the shallow lagoon. A dirt road ran past it, bordered by clumps of heavy bushes. No car was in sight.

Nan sighed. "Well, I guess that's that. Nobody's here."

Splash! Something was moving inside the tunnel!

CHAPTER XV

DOWN IN THE WELL!

THE STARTLED children peered into the tunnel.

"It's the bad men!" exclaimed Flossie as two figures appeared out of the shadows. They splashed through the shallow water toward the other end of the tunnel.

"We must catch them!" Henry exclaimed.

"No. Wait!" cried Nan. "We promised Aunt Doris we wouldn't go after them."

"Come back, Henry," Nellie put in. "We'll call the Lebanon police and tell them that Skinny and Fox are around here."

"I wonder where their car is," said Bert.

Nan pointed to the heavy brush along the road. "It's probably parked in the bushes. But what were they doing in the tunnel?"

Bert chuckled. "I think Flossie chased 'em there."

"Me!" exclaimed his little sister.

"Sure. You were talking about policemen on the way down, and they probably thought we were bringing the police."

The children giggled.

"It must be awfully icky in that water," said Nellie. "They'll have scum up to their knees."

The little group was still grinning when they reached the top of the path again. They pedaled back to town, turned in the bicycles and walked to the motel. Aunt Doris was in the lobby.

"Any luck?" she asked eagerly.

"Not much," said Nellie and explained what had happened.

"You were right not to go after the men," Mrs. Zoop said approvingly. "I'll call the police."

She gave the children the keys to their rooms and told them she had bought some clean clothing for them.

After dinner Bert and Nan asked the desk clerk if the Bartons had arrived. He checked the register.

"No one of that name is here."

The twins joined Nellie and Henry.

"What do we do now?" Nellie asked.

"I have an idea," Bert answered. "Let's stake out the lobby in case they come."

For the rest of the evening the four took turns sitting by the front doors, but did not see the tourist couple. Finally the children went to bed.

Early the next morning Bert and Nan took up their posts again in the deserted lobby. A young woman was on duty at the desk.

"My, such early birds," she said, stifling a yawn. "What kind of worms do you expect to catch?"

Nan smiled. "We're just watching for somebody."

Suddenly the elevator door opened and a man and a woman stepped out. Both were blond.

"Bert!" whispered Nan. "There they are!"

Quickly the twins crossed the lobby and waited near the desk while the man paid his bill. When he turned away, the twins stepped over. Bert introduced himself and Nan, then explained about the hex signs.

"They were stolen from your friend!" exclaimed Mrs. Barton. "Well, of course you may have them back!"

"Come with us to the car," her husband said. "We'll give the signs to you now."

On the way Nan told how they had gone to the Union Tunnel looking for the couple.

"That's too bad," Mrs. Barton said, "because we had decided not to go there after all. We spent the rest of the day with friends and didn't arrive at the motel until nearly midnight."

When they reached the Bartons' car, the man

unlocked the trunk and took out the two hex signs. He handed the old one to Nan and the other to Bert.

"We'll buy them from you," Bert offered. "How much did you pay the peddler?"

"Just keep them," said Mr. Barton, smiling.

The Bobbseys thanked him. A few moments later the couple drove off.

Excited and happy, the twins ran back to the motel. As they entered the lobby the rest of their group was just coming out of the elevator.

"Look what we found!" cried Nan as she and Bert held up the signs.

With a chorus of excited questions the others surrounded the older twins. Quickly they told their story.

"That's marvelous!" Aunt Doris exclaimed.

Henry looked a little sad. "I wish I'd been there," he said.

"Don't worry, Henry," said Nan cheerfully. "This mystery is far from solved. You'll have plenty of chances to do it."

After breakfast Aunt Doris explored the town with the children. At ten o'clock the station wagon was ready.

Bert put the big hex sign in the back of the car. Nan kept the old sign in her hands.

"Since we're here," said Aunt Doris as she took the wheel, "I think I'll stop at the Lebanon market."

Half an hour later she had finished shopping, and they set off again. Nan still held the old hex sign on her lap.

"I can't wait to see what it'll look like when it's cleaned," Nellie said. "Do you really think it'll have a clue to the secret passage on it?"

"I hope so," Nan replied.

After a while Aunt Doris suggested that they stop for a picnic lunch. "I just bought plenty of good Lebanon bologna and homemade rolls."

"Let's eat in Footer's Grove," Henry said eagerly. "May we, Mother, please?"

"Why not?" she replied. "It's on our way."

Before long Aunt Doris turned down a dirt road and pulled into a weed-grown driveway. Here and there among the trees the children could see wooden tables and benches. Some distance away in a clearing was a tumbledown frame house.

"What is that place over there?" Flossie asked.

"That's the Footer farmhouse," Henry said. "The family hasn't lived here for years. They rent the grounds to the county for a picnic grove."

"Let's eat over there!" Nan suggested. She laid the hex sign on the seat and skipped ahead of the others. She found a table under a large shady tree. Mrs. Zoop spread paper napkins for a cloth and the girls began making sandwiches.

"There are paper cups for the milk in the glove compartment," Aunt Doris said to Flossie. "Will you get them, dear?"

Flossie ran toward the car. As she darted among the trees into the driveway, the little girl stopped with a gasp. There was Skinny Broome!

"Oh!" Flossie squealed.

The next moment she saw Dr. Fox. He was stepping out of the front seat of the station wagon and had the old hex sign in his hand.

"Put that down!" Flossie cried. "It's not yours!"

Fox turned with a growl. "Keep away from me, kid!" he snapped.

"Help! Help! The bad men are stealing the sign!" Flossie screamed, racing toward the picnic table.

At the sound of her cries the whole party dropped what they were doing and sped over to the driveway.

"There they go!" Nan exclaimed, spotting the men running among the trees.

"They'll head for their car," said Bert. "It must be out on the road. Let's cut them off!"

Mrs. Zoop and the children broke ranks and swiftly circled around in front of the men. Skinny and Fox turned tail and raced back through the woods, dodging this way and that. They loped across the clearing.

Yelling, the young detectives pounded after

"Put that down!" Flossie cried. "It's not yours!"

them. Clutching the hex sign, Fox darted around the farmhouse. The children separated and circled it. They cornered him on the ramshackle porch.

"Give us back that sign!" Bert demanded.

Fox's black eyes flickered warily, but he did not move.

Aunt Doris came running up. "Don't you dare hurt those children!" she cried.

"You stole that sign!" Bert accused. "Give it back!"

"Don't you do it, Fox!" called Skinny as he dashed around the corner. He ran to a stone well in front of the porch. "Throw it to me!"

Instantly Fox tossed the sign over the children's heads. Skinny jumped for it, but the sign fell short. It went straight down into the well!

Nan gasped. For an instant everybody was too shocked to speak. Fox exploded, "You've lost it, you idiot!"

"Now no one has the clue!" Nan wailed.

Skinny was already fleeing among the trees. Fox leaped the broken porch rail and followed.

"Catch them!" Freddie shouted.

"It's no use," said Bert. "The sign's gone."

Aunt Doris and the others looked into the well. It was too dark to see the bottom.

"How'll we ever get the sign back?" Flossie asked.

"Maybe the owner of the property would give

us permission to go down for it," Bert said.

Mrs. Zoop nodded. "We'll call him as soon as we get home."

Sadly, they all went back to the picnic table. Their appetites were gone and they ate only a little. Soon they headed for Cloverbank.

When they told Uncle Walter what had happened, he telephoned Mr. Footer. After a brief conversation he hung up.

"Footer says we may go down into the well if we want to. I'll take you older children over there tonight and we'll see what we can do about getting the sign up," he promised.

"Can't we do it now?" Bert asked. "Skinny and Fox may get the sign first."

"I'm sorry, Bert," Mr. Zoop said. "I have a couple of sick sheep in the barn and can't leave until the vet comes. He'll be here after supper."

It was dusk by the time Uncle Walter could get away. Bert and Henry helped him load a long, collapsible ladder into the back of the station wagon as well as several coils of rope and a searchlight.

"I wish we could go too," said Freddie wistfully when the older children settled into the car with their flashlights.

Aunt Doris put her arms around the young twins. "It might be dangerous," she said. "You'll have a good time here. We'll make some fudge."

Freddie and Flossie cheered up and waved as

the others drove off. It was dark when they reached Footer's place. Uncle Walter parked on the shoulder of the road and switched off the lights.

"Now everybody go quietly," he said. "No use advertising that we're here."

Silently they unloaded the station wagon. Carrying their gear, the five picked their way through the moonlit grove to the edge of the clearing.

"We'd better stick to the woods," Uncle Walter whispered.

Keeping hidden, the detectives circled the farmhouse. When they reached the front, Bert stopped short.

"Look!" he whispered, pointing through the trees. A glow of light was coming up out of the well!

CHAPTER XVI

THE BLACK HOLE

THE Cloverbank group watched silently from the edge of the woods. Suddenly Fox appeared from the shadows and looked down into the lighted well.

"Did you find it?" he called softly.

Skinny's voice came up hollowly, and the listeners could not understand what he said. A few moments later he climbed out of the well. In one hand he held a muddy disk!

"If you ask me we ought to forget about the secret passage," he grumbled. "It's too dangerous."

"Don't worry," Fox replied. "Nobody would think to look for us around here. As soon as we find that golden gift we'll pick up the big loot and clear out." He pulled up a rope ladder and light.

Meanwhile Bert had been thinking quickly.

He signaled the others and they slipped back into the woods.

"Why don't we tackle 'em?" Henry whispered eagerly. "There are five of us."

"I've another idea," said Bert. As the others bent their heads closer he softly told his plan.

"Good idea, boy," said Uncle Walter.

Following instructions, the children scattered among the trees in front of the farmhouse. While the two men were packing up their gear, Bert gave a long low whistle. The prowlers froze.

"What was that?" Fox snapped.

Skinny said nothing, but his eyes rolled wildly as he looked around him. The next moment Nan cracked a twig loudly. At this, Nellie, some distance away, rustled the brush. Then Henry crushed more twigs and Uncle Walter returned Bert's whistle.

"There's somebody in the woods," said Skinny hoarsely. "A whole lot of them!"

Suddenly Uncle Walter beamed his powerful searchlight on the two men and shouted, "All right, you two! Put down that sign! You're surrounded!"

"Police!" shrilled Skinny and dropped the hex sign.

He dashed for the woods with Fox at his heels. When they disappeared, the children burst into the yard. Nan quickly picked up the sign.

"That was a keen idea!" exclaimed Henry. "Did you see how scared they were?"

Uncle Walter chuckled. "We got the hex sign back, and those two fellows had to do all the work!"

"Did you hear them mention 'big loot'?" Nan asked eagerly. "I'll bet they *are* the hotel robbers." Quickly she told Uncle Walter what the young twins had heard from the barber.

"You're probably right," said Mr. Zoop. "I'll pass this on to the police."

"Where do you suppose they hid the loot?" Nellie asked.

"Who knows?" Henry asked. "There are hundreds of places around here."

Talking excitedly about their adventure, the group hurried to their car.

"Let's take the hex sign to Otto now," Bert suggested.

Uncle Walter agreed. After calling the police from a pay station, he drove straight to Hummel's barn.

When the artist opened the door he beamed. *"Ach,* company! Come in and have a *sitz,"* he said, leading them to the big table.

Nan held out the muddy sign. "We got back the old Cloverbank hex sign, Otto. Would you please clean it so we can see if it is the clue to the secret passage?"

Otto's eyebrows shot up and he exchanged looks with Uncle Walter. "Well, now, you are really some smart detectives!"

"I'll say they are!" said Mr. Zoop.

While the children told their story, Otto wiped the mud off the sign. Then he poured a special fluid onto a piece of cotton and carefully began to rub the old dirt off the wood.

The visitors watched eagerly over his shoulders as faded green leaves were revealed in the center.

"A four-leaf clover!" Nellie exclaimed.

"What's that on the edge?" Nan asked, when a red-and-yellow pointed design appeared.

"Looks like flames to me," said Bert.

"Oh!" his twin exclaimed. "You know what they might stand for? The fireplace in the mystery room! Maybe the entrance to the secret passage is there after all!"

Excitedly the others agreed.

"We'd better go home and examine the fireplace right away," said Nellie.

Twenty minutes later the Zoops and all their visitors were in the mystery room. Once more they examined the fireplace, stone by stone. Not one was loose.

Henry frowned. "There's no opening here."

"Maybe the hex sign doesn't have a meaning after all," said Nellie with a sigh.

Everyone was disppointed.

"Well, anyway, our fudge turned out yummy," Flossie spoke up.

After eating some of the creamy chocolate squares, the children went to bed. Next morning at breakfast they heard a light rapping on the screen door. The family looked up to see Amos Shrucker and his little sister standing there. Quickly Aunt Doris opened the door.

"Come in, please," she said, smiling. Amos and Rachel stepped inside shyly, and Henry introduced them to his parents.

"We just came to invite the children to our feast this noon," said Amos. "They were so nice to help us with the buggy."

Flossie clapped her hands. "Oh, we'd love to come!" The other children beamed and agreed.

Amos blushed. "Eleven o'clock," he said, and told them how to find his home. "Come, Rachel."

The little girl had been standing close beside him, eyeing Flossie shyly.

"Good-by," she whispered and went out, still clinging to her brother's hand.

"You can go in the pony cart," said Uncle Walter. "Aunt Doris and I will take the car and spend the afternoon in town."

Promptly at eleven Daisy trotted into a farmyard filled with Amish buggies. Henry pulled up beside the white stone house.

Amos and Rachel hurried out to greet the visitors, and led them into the big kitchen to meet their mother. She was a stout, pink-faced woman wearing a blue dress and white cap. Smiling pleasantly, she wiped her hands on her apron, then shook the hand of each child.

"Now you go out in the yard," she said, "and eat yourselves full."

The visitors followed the Shruckers to a long table under the trees. Bearded men in wide black hats and dark suits were standing around talking.

Amos introduced the visitors to his older sister, a tall, blond girl named Martha. She sat with them at dinner.

"I never saw so much food!" Nan exclaimed.

There were mashed potatoes mixed with celery, meat loaf, hot slaw, ham, fried chicken, and homemade bread with several jams and jellies. Flossie bit into a large pickle and pursed her mouth.

Rachel giggled. "It's wonderful sour!"

"But wait till you eat shoofly pie." Henry said, grinning. "That's wonderful sweet!"

When everything had been cleared away, the women brought six large brown pies to the table. They had warm molasses filling on top of their crumbly crust.

"But I don't see any flies," said Freddie.

"That is chust a nickname," Martha told him.

"It's yummy!" Flossie cried out after tasting her first delicious morsel.

Afterward Amos showed the children around. Rachel and Flossie trailed behind the others, hand in hand, talking happily.

In the parlor Amos said, "Do you notice we have no curtains or rugs? That's because we Amish do not believe in having decorations."

"You have lots of flowers, though," said Nan, admiring the geraniums on each window sill.

"Oh, yes," Martha said with a smile. "But those are natural decorations. God made those."

"Is your house very old?" Bert asked curiously. He had noticed the thick, whitewashed stone walls.

"Yes," Amos replied. "The Shruckers have been on this farm for over a hundred years."

"Then maybe you could help us with our mystery," said Nan and explained about the secret passage and the prowlers.

"We don't know anything about Cloverbank," said Amos regretfully.

"Maybe this would help," Martha spoke up. She went to a large chest of drawers and pulled out a big envelope. From it she took a worn parchment and spread it on the table.

"It's a map—all hand drawn!" exclaimed Bert as he bent over it eagerly.

"This was made just before the Revolution," said Amos.

"There are little drawings on it," exclaimed Nellie. "Look at the tiny trees and the river and the mill!"

"Here's our place," Henry told them, pointing to the picture of a house and barn with *Cloverbank* printed underneath in faded ink.

"But there's something wrong with it," said Nellie. "It doesn't look right."

"It's this chimney," said Nan, pointing to the one nearest the barn. "Here it's on the very end of the house. But now that chimney is between the end room and the next one."

"I see!" said Bert excitedly. "A wing has been added to the house!"

Nan gasped. "That means the mystery room is not the last one any more, but is now *second* from the end!"

"You mean we've been searching the wrong room?" Nellie asked in amazement.

"That's right," said Bert.

Amos' eyes were sparkling with excitement. "Go right away," he said, "and look in the real mystery room."

"Yes, don't wait," said Martha. "We understand."

Quickly the visitors thanked all the Shruckers for the feast, then drove swiftly home. Leaving Daisy and the cart in the backyard, the young-

The iron piece moved sideways

sters hurried onto the porch. Henry unlocked the door and they hastened upstairs to the real mystery room. It was a spare bedroom with one window.

Bert ran to the fireplace, knelt down and looked in. The back wall of it was a black iron plate with a heavy ring in the center. He seized the ring and pushed and pulled. The plate did not budge.

"Maybe it slides," Nan suggested.

Bert jerked on the ring and with a grating sound the iron piece moved sideways.

Behind it was a black hole! On the far side was the stone wall of the chimney. Fastened to this was an iron ladder. It led down into the darkness.

"The secret passage!" Nellie exclaimed. "We've found it!"

"What are we waiting for?" Henry cried excitedly. "Let's go down that ladder!"

CHAPTER XVII

TWO TREASURES

"WAIT a minute," said Bert. He sat back on his heels and looked at the dark opening in the fireplace. "I don't understand how this secret passage worked."

"What do you mean?" Nellie asked. "The people just went down the ladder into the hole."

"But what if there was a fire? They couldn't crawl through that," said Bert.

"You're right! I forgot about that," said Nellie.

Nan spoke up. "When the Hessian soldier disappeared, there were logs burning in the fireplace."

Flossie had crept alongside of Bert and was peering into the hole. "Look! What's that?" She pointed to a long object wedged between the stone chimney and the ladder.

"Looks like a box," said Bert. He reached down and managed to pry out the rusty container. With his pocketknife he forced up the lid. Inside were some long thin pieces of wood, a small patch of linen and several flints.

"What is all that stuff?" Freddie wanted to know.

"People used this to start a fire before matches were invented," Nan replied. She explained that the flint was struck to make sparks which were caught in the cloth. "Then the person blew on them to produce a flame to light the sticks."

Bert's eyes were sparkling. "I see now how the trick was worked! Wood must have been ready in the fireplace all the time. When the soldier escaped he crawled over it and down into the hole. Then he hung onto the ladder, lit the fire and closed the iron plate!"

Nan grinned. "And the British never dreamed he was back there!"

"Let's go down in the hole," Henry said eagerly.

"Right away," Bert replied and sent the young twins to get flashlights.

A few minutes later he grasped the ladder and started down into the darkness. The girls came next, then Freddie and Henry. It seemed a long time before they reached the last rung and turned on their lights. Before them was the mouth of a narrow tunnel.

"We must be below the cellar," said Bert. His voice echoed eerily.

Filing into the passage, the young detectives flashed their lights around and saw a low, rocky ceiling held up by heavy timbers. The stones glistened with dampness.

"It's cold," said Flossie, shivering.

The six walked on without talking. Their footsteps echoed strangely.

"Careful here," Bert called back. "There are a lot of broken stones around."

"I guess they fell from the roof," said Nan, glancing up uneasily.

As the children stepped over the chunks of rock, there was a loud clatter.

"Ow!" exclaimed Nellie softly. "I kicked a stone."

"Don't make so much noise," Henry told his cousin.

"What difference does it make?" Nellie replied. "There's nobody to hear us."

"Who knows what's down here?" he said. "It's spooky."

Suddenly Bert stopped. "Hold it!" he exclaimed. "I've found something!"

The children gathered around him and looked down at a pile of moldy cloth.

"Why it's a soldier's uniform!" Nan cried out. She stooped beside it. "See, here's a metal button. That's pewter, I think," she added. "See how it's turned black with age."

"I'll bet this was the Hessian's uniform," said Henry.

"My guess is that the Scott children gave him some other clothes for a disguise," Nan suggested, "and he changed into them here."

"This uniform's historical," said Nellie. "I'm sure Miss Lulu at the Old-Time House would love to have it."

"We can pick it up on the way back," said Bert.

"I wish we'd find the golden birthday present," Flossie put in.

"If we do," said Freddie, "we'll just have one mystery left to solve—who was trying to dig up the four-leaf clovers?"

"And why?" Nan added. "That's what I can't figure out."

The children stepped around the ancient clothes and continued along the tunnel. As thcy walked in silence, Bert puzzled over Nan's question.

Suddenly he stopped and said, "Listen, everybody! I have an idea! Remember the day we went to the Lancaster market? The cheese man told us Dr. Fox had gone to the flower stall."

"So what?" asked Henry.

"There were clumps of four-leaf clover for sale at that stand! Maybe Fox bought two and planted them in your sheep meadow."

"It's a soldier's uniform!" Nan cried

"But why would he do that?" Nellie asked in amazement.

"I know!" Nan answered, her eyes sparkling. She had guessed her twin's thought. "To mark the places where he buried the hotel loot!"

"But why were the clumps partly out of the ground?" Flossie questioned.

Bert frowned. "The men may have dug up the money and taken it away."

"Let's go to the clover bank and see if the loot is gone," said Freddie eagerly.

"We will," Bert promised, "as soon as we find out where this tunnel leads."

Excited by their new idea, the children hurried on. Suddenly Henry, who was last in line, paused. He thought he had heard a noise somewhere behind him.

Henry whispered to Freddie to pass the message to the head of the line. When it reached Bert, he stopped.

"Listen!" he said softly.

The children stood quietly. They heard the drop of water from the rocks overhead and the scurrying of something small in the shadows.

"What did you hear, Henry?" Nan whispered.

"It sounded like somebody kicking a stone."

"Maybe Uncle Walter and Aunt Doris came home and found the fireplace open and they've followed us," Nellie suggested.

Before Bert could stop him, Freddie called, "Uncle Walter! Is that you?"

There was no answer.

"It was probably just a mouse," said Nellie.

Bert frowned. "Let's not make any more noise than we have to," he said uneasily.

Quietly the detectives went on. Suddenly Bert stopped, and Nan gave a gasp of alarm.

"What's the matter?" Nellie cried.

A moment later the older twins laughed. "It's just something wrapped in leather," said Nan, pointing to a niche in the wall.

"It startled me for a moment too," Bert added.

As the others held their lights on the object, Bert lifted it out and began to unwrap the leather.

"What is it? What's inside?" Freddie asked eagerly, trying to peer between the older children.

"A box!" Henry exclaimed.

The package was wrapped in brown paper. Across the outside of it in fancy handwriting were the words: Hummel *Kinder*.

"What does that mean?" Freddie asked.

"Hummel children," Henry answered.

"It's the birthday present!" Nan exclaimed.

"Open it!" Flossie begged.

"No," said Nan quickly. "It belongs to Otto. He'll have to open it."

"A golden present!" said Flossie. "I can't wait to see it."

"Let's take it with us," Nan suggested. "If we can get out the other end of the tunnel, we can go straight to Otto's and find out what's in the box."

"That's cool," said Henry. "Then we'll dig up the clover."

Nan took the box and they walked on. Suddenly Bert said, "This is the end."

He stopped and the others saw that they had reached a solid rock wall. Two rough steps had been cut into it.

Bert aimed his light at the ceiling. "There's a trapdoor!"

He climbed up the stairs and pushed hard at the wooden panel. It did not budge.

"We might need a crowbar for this," he muttered.

"There's no telling how many years since it was opened," Nan murmured.

"Here, take my flashlight," said Henry. "You can use the handle to pound with."

Bert took the light and began to beat it against the trapdoor. After a few moments the wood moved slightly.

"I think I'm getting it!" he said breathlessly, and gave another hard knock. "Yes! Here it comes!"

As he pushed upward, there was a loud creaking and a shower of dirt and dust fell down. The children peered up as daylight streamed into the tunnel.

"Where does it come out?" Flossie asked.

Bert stuck his head outside and Nan climbed up beside him. "In the woods near the barn," he said.

The next moment there was the sound of running footsteps in the tunnel. The children aimed their lights into the darkness. Fox and Skinny were racing toward them! Before the surprised children could move, the men were up to them.

"This time we've got you!" growled Fox. "Hand over that box!"

CHAPTER XVIII

WONDERFUL GOOD FUN!

FOR a moment the children were too frightened to speak. Then Nan clutched the birthday present tighter.

"We're not going to give you anything, Dr. Fox," she said. "After all, there are six of us and only two of you."

The big man took a sudden step forward, seized Nan and swung her off the steps.

"Stop that!" cried Bert and leaped down the stairs toward him.

But Fox sidestepped neatly and Bert went sprawling on the floor of the tunnel. As Henry went after him, Skinny jerked the box from Nan and bounded up the steps toward the open trapdoor.

"You come back with that!" cried Freddie, seizing Skinny's shirt.

Flossie and Nellie also grabbed for the peddler, but he broke free and dashed outside. Fox pushed past the children and followed.

"After them!" cried Bert, rushing up the steps.

The children quickly climbed out. The two men were running toward the barn.

"Cut them off! Stop them!" Henry yelled, as they all dashed after the thieves.

"Shoo 'em around to the pit!" Nan called.

Sprinting hard, the children tore to the front of the barn just as the two men rounded the opposite corner.

"Yow!" yelped Skinny and turned tail.

"Run!" cried Fox as the screeching children chased them behind the building.

A moment later both men stepped on the crossed branches. With wild yells and waving arms they disappeared from sight.

"Yippee! We've caught them!" Henry shouted and the others joined in the excitement.

Bert tossed aside the few branches that were left and the young detectives peered into the pit. Skinny was seated on the ground looking up dazedly. Fox got to his feet. He waved both fists when he saw the children.

"Get us out of here!" he roared.

"Toss up that birthday present and we'll see about it," said Bert.

The big man's eyes glinted angrily. "I will not!"

"Yippee, we've caught them!" Henry shouted

"Give them the present," said Skinny in a shaky voice, "or they might call the cops."

"All right," said Fox. He picked up the box from the ground and tossed it up to Bert. "Now get us out of here."

"In a little while," Bert replied.

"I mean right now!" Fox bellowed furiously.

"First you have to answer some questions for us," said Bert firmly.

Fuming, Fox turned to Skinny and jerked him to his feet. "You! Climb on my shoulders and get out of here. Then help me up."

"Come on, Skinny," said Henry with a grin. He picked up one of the stout limbs which had been lying across the pit. "As soon as you poke your head over the edge, I'll whack you with this—*pow!*"

Skinny groaned. "Tell them what they want to know, Fox. Maybe they'll let us out then."

Meanwhile Nan had whispered something to the young twins. They dashed off toward the clover bank.

"How did you find the tunnel?" Bert asked the men.

"We sneaked in the house to search that mystery room again," said Fox hoarsely. "The door to the second room was open, and we saw the hole in the fireplace, so we went down."

"We could hear you ahead of us in the tunnel," Skinny added.

"How did you find out there was a golden birthday present?" Nellie asked Dr. Fox.

The big man said that he was not a professor or a writer, but an antique dealer. "Several weeks ago I bought an old desk at an auction in Lebanon," he explained. "Behind one of the drawers I found a letter that was never mailed. It was from John Hummel, thanking Uncle Fritz for a golden birthday gift. Hummel wrote that he had hidden it in a secret tunnel which he had just discovered in the Cloverbank house."

Skinny spoke up sadly. "It's too bad he didn't say where the passage was. We'd have been saved a lot of trouble."

Fox nodded. "I prowled around trying to find an outside exit to the tunnel, but I had no luck."

"Who made the dummy we found in the sheep meadow?" Bert wanted to know.

Fox said that Skinny had stolen the clothes from an Amish farmer and rigged up the figure. "We thought it would frighten you into minding your own business."

"The kids scared us more than we scared them," grumbled Skinny.

"Speak for yourself," said Fox sharply. "You were the chicken! Just because you heard the little girl mention the police you panicked. And what did we have to do? Hide in the canal tunnel!" He snorted in disgust.

"And you were some wonderful detective,

Fox!" retorted Skinny. "All the time you were looking in the wrong room for the secret passage. You and your corny disguises from the costume shop!"

As he spoke, the young twins came racing up. Each was carrying a metal box.

"We found the loot!" Freddie boasted. "One box under each clump of four-leaf clovers."

Loud groans came from the pit.

"I told you not to bury it there!" wailed Skinny.

"Be quiet!" Fox commanded.

"It's too late," said Skinny. "They know everything!" He told the children that Fox was really a robber and just had a little antique business on the side. "I met Fox last month at an auction," the peddler added. "He talked me into robbing the hotel with him."

Meanwhile Bert and Nan had opened the boxes. Each was full of money. Fox said he had hidden them separately for safety and marked the spots with lucky clover as Bert had guessed.

"We dug the patches up once to be sure the boxes were still there," said Skinny sadly. "I should have taken them away then."

"You didn't put the clover back straight," said Flossie. "That's how we knew there was something funny about them."

Just then the hum of a car could be heard in the driveway.

Henry jumped up. "I hope it's Mother and Dad!" he cried. "I'll go see."

Twenty minutes later the police arrived. The six children, Aunt Doris and Uncle Walter watched quietly as four officers hauled the two disheveled men out of the pit. The thieves stood scowling with leaves and twigs in their hair while Bert told what had happened. Then he handed over the stolen money.

"Thanks," said one of the policemen. "Lucky for you youngsters that this animal trap was here."

"That's not for animals. It's a Prowler's Pit," Bert said. "It was Henry's idea. He made it."

"That was a great idea, son! It came in very handy," said the officer and Henry beamed proudly.

The policeman smiled at all the children. "You've certainly done a big day's work!"

Aunt Doris put one arm around her son and the other around Nan. "I'm proud of all our detectives."

The police loaded Skinny and Fox into the squad car. As it sped down the highway, Nan ran inside to telephone Otto and tell him the good news.

In a short time his old truck came rattling up the drive. The brakes squealed, and he jumped down.

"Where is it?" he cried eagerly.

Nan ran over with the package. Hardly able to believe his eyes, Otto took it from her. He carried it to the back porch and sat on the steps near the pony cart. Everyone clustered around.

As Otto fumbled with the strings, Jiffy Jay flapped down from his perch and sat on Henry's head. Sheela stuck her nose through the wires of her pen, and Daisy turned to watch.

"The animals want to see the present too," Flossie said.

"Uncle Fritz wrote that it was something special for Pennsylvania children," Nan reminded them. "I just can't wait to see it!"

Otto removed the paper and laid it aside. In his hands was a wooden box. He lifted the brass latch on the front and raised the lid.

"Oh!" cried Flossie and Nan caught her breath.

Glistening in the sunlight were ten little golden birds seated on a golden branch.

"Distelfinks!" Nellie exclaimed.

"It's bee-yoo-ti-ful!" said Flossie.

Carefully Otto lifted out the branch and they saw that it was mounted on a brass box.

"It's a bank!" Henry exclaimed. He pointed to a small slot in front of each bird. "See, that's where the money goes into the box!"

"Let's see if it works," Nan exclaimed.

Bert took out a nickel and slipped it in one of the slots. As the coin clinked into the bank, the bird bent forward and popped up again. Then all ten began to sing.

"It's a music box too!" said Nellie and the others exclaimed in delight.

"What are you going to do with it, Otto?" Henry asked.

"I think it ought to go to Miss Lulu at the Old-Time House," the artist replied. "It will be safe there and everyone can enjoy it."

Flossie danced a little jig. "Won't Miss Lulu be surprised when she gets this and the uniform, too!"

Otto stood up. "Yes, and there are more surprises coming. Wait until tomorrow at the Farm Show!"

Next morning at breakfast, Henry's father invited the children to ride in the covered wagon in the opening parade. They agreed happily.

Uncle Walter said, "As soon as you get to the fairgrounds, go to the dressing tent. Miss Lulu will be there, and she'll give you pioneer costumes. Then hurry to the big meadow and get into the Conestoga."

An hour later the Bobbseys and their friends were settled in the front of the wagon with Bert holding the reins of the six white horses. The girls wore large sunbonnets and long calico dresses. The boys had on coonskin caps with deerskin jackets and pants.

Lined up behind them were horseback riders,

twirlers, and a brass band. A happy crowd surrounded the meadow, waiting for the parade to begin.

Suddenly Otto appeared beside the children with a large box and a microphone. "Ladies and gentlemen," he boomed, "these are the Bobbsey twins, Nellie Parks, and Henry Zoop. They are the young detectives you heard about on the news broadcast this morning, who solved the mystery." The people applauded. "I have some presents for them."

He reached into the box and took out two copies of the old Cloverbank hex sign. He presented one to Henry and one to Nellie. Both children beamed and thanked him.

Then he took out a very large hex sign which he held up for everyone to see. In the center were twin birds facing one another. Between them was a big red B.

"It's a double *distelfink* sign," he announced. "It means good luck for the Bobbseys." He pointed to two bright red hearts at the bottom. "These stand for their courage and kindness."

The twins blushed happily as Bert accepted the sign from Otto.

"I'm sorry our four-leaf-clover mystery's over," said Freddie. "It was such fun."

"Yes," said Nan, smiling. "It was a real Pennsylvania Dutch mystery—wonderful good!"